ROSA

Elaine Cunningham

A Beka Book® Pensacola, FL 32523-9100
an affiliate of PENSACOLA CHRISTIAN COLLEGE®

Rosa

Illustrator: Dave Apling

Copyright ©1991 Pensacola Christian College
All rights reserved. Printed in U.S.A. 2008 C04

No part of this publication may be reproduced or transmitted in any form or by any means, electronic or mechanical, including photocopy, recording, or any information storage and retrieval system, or by license from any collective or licensing body, without permission in writing from the publisher.

Cataloging Data
Cunningham, Elaine.
    Rosa/ Elaine Cunningham
    107 p.: col. ill.; 24 cm.— (A Beka Book reading program)
    1. Readers. 2. Reading. I. A Beka Book, Inc.
 Library of Congress: PE1119 .C86 R67 1991
 Dewey System: 428.6

CHAPTERS

1. The Cabin   3
2. A New Friend   17
3. The Christian School   31
4. The Program   45
5. The Rattlesnake   59
6. The Picnic   73
7. Rosa to the Rescue   83
8. A Friend Forever   95

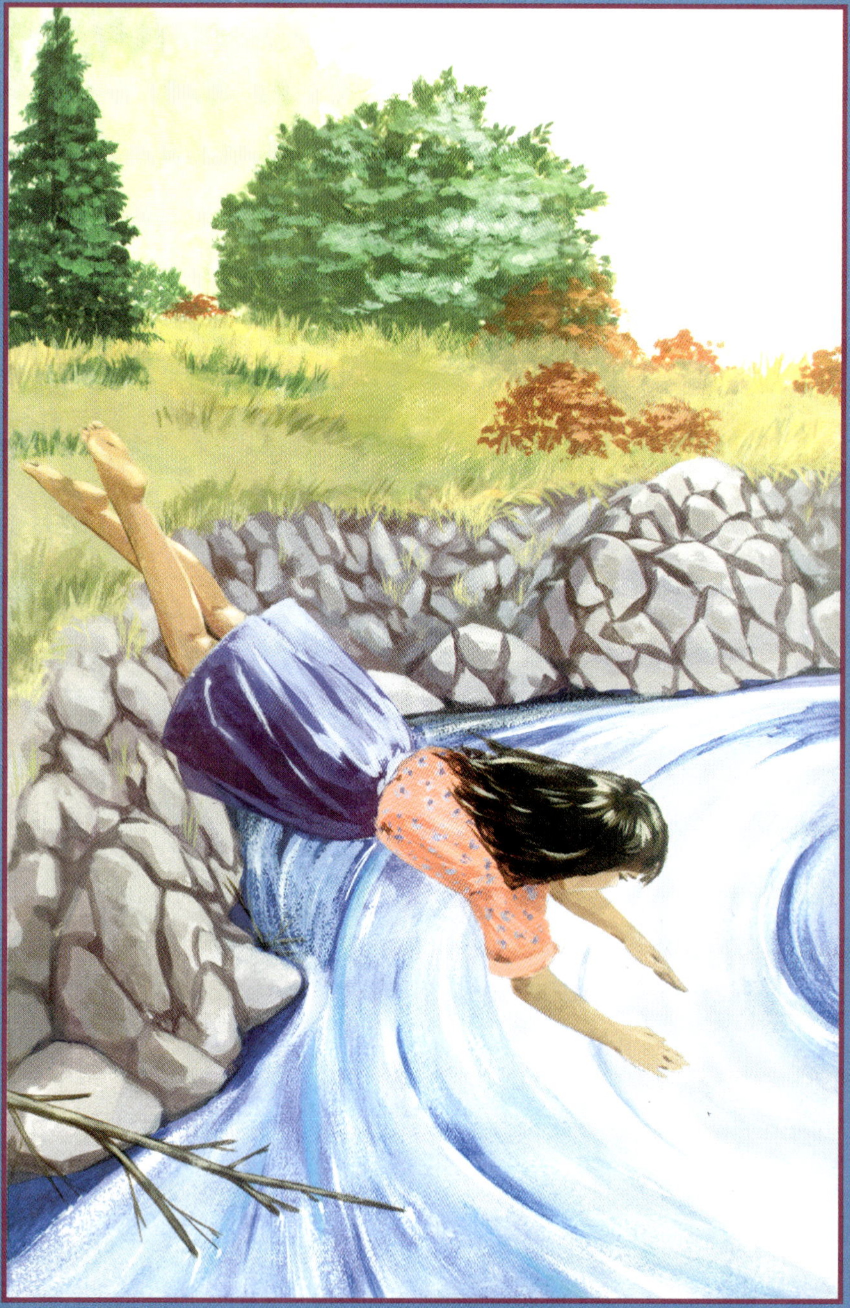

Author's Note

    Although the story of Rosa is fiction, it is located in a very real setting. At the time I wrote the book I lived in the beautiful Yakima Valley located in the eastern part of Washington State. Several children who were of Mexican descent attended the church which my husband pastored. We loved them dearly.

    With an orchard owner's permission, I visited his migrant cabins and interviewed him to get firsthand information about the migrant workers who come each year to help harvest his apple crop.

    Many thanks are also due to Deborah Mayberry who lives in the Yakima Valley. She gave me much local information, walked the river setting with me, and helped with Spanish phrases and cultural information.

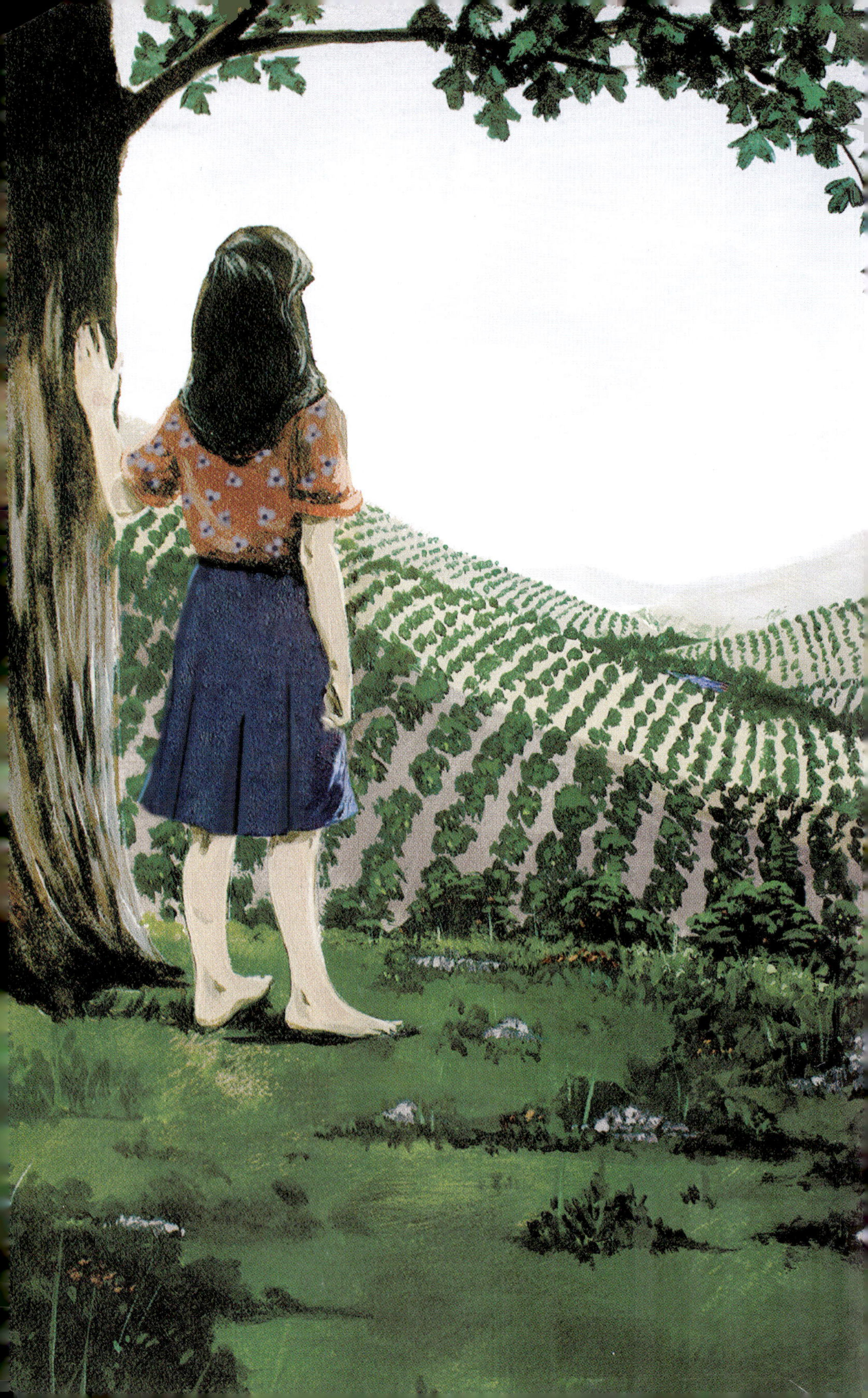

Chapter One

THE CABIN

Apple trees covered the sloping hillsides as far as Rosa could see. Red apples, golden apples—rows of trees spread in every direction. Beyond the orchard, at the bottom of the hill, the river ran like a silver thread through the valley. Twelve-year-old Rosa was a tall girl with light brown skin and long black hair. Her dark eyes stared unseeingly at the beauty surrounding her. Suddenly she sank to the dusty ground and let the tears come.

"How can I go to school again looking this way?" She yanked at her ragged cotton skirt. "Stupid old raggedy thing!" She stuck her bare, calloused feet out in front of her. "If only I had some pretty dresses and cute outfits like the other girls . . . If I just had my own bedroom. . . . If I lived in a real house, instead of a shack. . . . If I could just stay in one school for a full year. . . . If I had a friend. . . . If. . . . If. . . . If. . . ." The tears ran down her cheeks.

"Rosa, come here." *Mamá's* shrill voice carried to the top of the hill. "Come fix the tortillas for supper." Rosa scrambled to her feet and wiped her face with the back of her hand. A clean streak showed on her hand. "How did I get so dirty?" she said to herself. "I shouldn't have sat in the dirt. *Mamá* will really be upset." Rosa brushed off the back of her skirt, took one last look across the valley, and hurried down the hill.

Rosa's new home was the Yakima Valley in Washington State. Last week it was the Hood River Valley in Oregon. The only difference—rows of apple trees instead of pears.

School was the hardest part. Rosa hated going into a new classroom every few weeks. She was always behind in math, always trying to catch up in reading, always struggling with spelling, always trying to find a friend.

Yesterday, when they arrived, she had overheard *Papá* telling *Mamá* that it was the tenth day of September. "Rosa needs to get started in school," he said. Right then Rosa had decided that she wasn't going to go to school anymore.

Mamá looked at Rosa's face as she neared the cabin. "Why are tears running down your cheeks?" she asked.

"*No es nada,*" Rosa said. "I mean, it's nothing. I'm trying to remember to speak English." She turned toward her mother. *Mamá* looked tired. Her black hair hung in strings around her sweaty face. "Oh, *Mamá,* I wish I didn't have to go to a new school always." Rosa stopped and wiped her eyes again. "You don't know what it's like to face all those new kids, and a new teacher, and try to catch up in everything."

"Be thankful you can go to school." *Mamá* spoke sharply. "I never had that chance."

"I know," Rosa said. "I do like to read and write and learn things, but. . . ." She looked past her mother, past the one-room cabin with its weatherbeaten brown paint and horseshoes nailed over the door. She tried to ignore the stained sofa that sat outside the shack, and the rusty van that carried her family from place to place. She stared down past the row of shacks, out toward the orchard. "It's just . . . oh, I can't explain." Wiping her face one more time on the sleeve of her blouse, she walked into the cabin.

Rosa smelled the spices that came from the pot of beans cooking on the back of the wood stove. The odor mingled with the smell of wet wood. *Mamá* must have mopped the wooden floor. Some boards were damp. No wonder *Mamá* looked so tired and sweaty! The cabin was as hot as an oven. Stepping carefully over the still-wet boards, Rosa followed her mother inside. Two-year-old Juan, just waking from a nap, kicked his bare feet over the side of the mattress, jumped off, and ran to Rosa. "Up, up," he said.

"I can't pick you up now, Juan. I have to fix the tortillas."

"Drink. Drink," Juan pleaded.

"Oh, all right. I'll get you a drink, if I can find a glass." Rosa rummaged in the box under the table until she found an empty jelly jar. Taking it to the bucket on the table, she quickly dipped out half a glass of water and handed it to the thirsty boy.

"Where's the basket for the tortillas, *Mamá?*" Rosa asked. "I need a clean towel, too."

"The towels are in the box next to the roll of bedding under the window," her mother said, with a deep sigh. "I haven't had time to unpack everything. Juan and Graciela are no help, and you went off to the orchard." She picked up Rosa's brother and placed him in the doorway. "Go, little one. Play outside in the sunshine with Graciela. You're in our way."

Rosa looked around the cabin. It was just like most of the others they had lived in. The walls were rough, unfinished boards with knotholes big enough to see through. Cardboard covered the ceiling, and a bare light bulb hung from a cord in the center of the room. Someone had nailed a cracker box to the wall above the table. It didn't look sturdy enough to hold anything very heavy. Maybe the salt and pepper and other spices could sit there.

A path of sunshine coming from the one window showed the meagerness of the furnishings in the room. An old iron bedstead with nothing on it but a thin mattress stood against one wall. Rosa knew that *Papá* and *Mamá* would sleep on the bed while she and the younger children slept on quilts on the floor that night. There was no other place. Rosa was glad that *Mamá* always strung a wire across the room and hung a sheet so she could have some privacy for dressing. *Mamá* also brought a piece of cardboard with her whenever she moved to another place. She put it over the window so no one could see inside at night.

The stove in one corner provided heat and a place to cook. There was a little door under the two round metal lids on the left. That was where you put the wood. The oven was on the other side of the stove, beneath the flat cooking surface.

Rosa read the name of the stove on the front door of the oven. "Midget." It was a good name for such a small stove. Grease spatters covered the wall beside the stove. The stovepipe went up from the back of the stove and disappeared in a metal ring in the cardboard ceiling. A fly strip, covered with flies, hung beside it.

As usual there wasn't a sink. Rosa knew that she would be carrying many buckets of water from the washhouse for cooking and for drinking.

A wooden table and chair sat in the middle of the room. There was a shelf beside the door for *Papá's* radio, and two other shelves for storing dishes. All the family clothes hung on six hooks on the wall. An old refrigerator completed the furnishings. At least this cabin was clean. Some places had been filthy before she and *Mamá* scoured them from top to bottom.

Rosa found the basket. The towel was in the big box, packed around some pottery. She removed the bucket of lard that *Mamá* had left on the table and poured some water into a pan to wash her hands.

Reaching into the large bowl of dough that *Mamá* had prepared, Rosa divided it into balls the size of small apples. She patted one into a flat circle. Rosa liked the feel of the dough. Soft and pliable, it fit inside her hand like the lump of clay she had once used in an art class at a school in California. She smacked it with the palm of her hand, stretching and pulling until it was paper thin.

Rosa knew that *Mamá* was proud of her tortillas. Most everyone bought tortillas at the store these days, but *Mamá* still made her dough. Rosa flopped the tortilla onto the hot stove lid. After a few seconds, she lifted one edge of the dough with her fingernail to check and see that it wasn't burning. Carefully she flipped it over, making sure that she didn't touch the hot stove with her fingers. One by one, Rosa did them all, laying them in the towel inside the large, flat basket when they were done. Then she folded the towel ends over the tortillas to keep them warm.

Mamá was busy trying to find something in which to cook the tomatoes and green peppers. "Where did I put that skillet?" she muttered. Her soft, dark eyes clouded over.

"Did you look out in the van?" Rosa asked. *Mamá* was always losing things. "I think we used it yesterday to fry beans, on the way here."

"You're right, we did," *Mamá* said. "What would I do without you?"

Rosa smiled. She loved *Mamá*. She loved *Mamá's* straight, black hair. When it was freshly washed it shone like a blackbird's wing. She loved *Mamá's* short, round body that was so easy to hug. She loved her brown eyes when they beamed with love. But sometimes *Mamá's* eyes pierced right through you. Then her tongue was sharp and cutting. Her scolding made you feel as worthless as a piece of tumbleweed. Then the next thing *Mamá* would be praising you and talking sweet. You never knew about *Mamá*.

"When is *Papá* coming in?" Rosa asked.

"He'll be here soon," *Mamá* said. "He's in the washroom taking a shower."

"Shall I holler outside the washroom and tell him supper's nearly ready?" Rosa asked.

"No, he wouldn't hear you with the water running." *Mamá* sighed. "They picked goldens today. Tomorrow I have to start picking too. I'll be as tired and dirty as he is." She looked at Rosa. "How did *you* get so dirty?"

"I climbed the little hill behind the cabins and sat on the ground in the orchard. It's dusty up there," she said.

"After supper you better take a shower so you'll be ready for school tomorrow. You may not have fancy clothes to wear, but you'll be clean as long as I have anything to say about it."

"*Mamá,* I don't want to go to school. Please don't make me." Tears brimmed up in Rosa's eyes again. "The kids call me an illegal alien. And I'll have to spend most of the day getting special help because I don't understand English very well."

Rosa put another plate on the table while she talked. "They make fun of my clothes, and they laugh when I bring refried beans for lunch. I feel like a crow in the middle of a bunch of parrots. All the other girls at school have pretty clothes, and they talk to each other so fast that I can't understand them. Please, *Mamá,* please let me stay home."

"No, Rosa, you must go to school. Do you want to be like me all your life? Can't read much English, always poor, always stuck in the orchards?"

"Rosa! Rosa! Come here!" Four-year-old Graciela called to her older sister.

"I can't. I'm helping *Mamá* get supper."

"You have to see this. Come quick." Graciela came inside and pulled at her sister's hand.

Rosa looked at her mother. *Mamá* nodded her head. "Go see what she wants. I'll watch the stove."

Scurrying through the door, Rosa followed Graciela and Juan past two cabins, past the washroom with its shower, sink, and toilet, and then past three more cabins. Rosa hadn't been down at this end of the property. She noticed that the other cabins were still empty. Padlocks hung outside the doors.

"That's good," Rosa said. "Our family will be the only ones using the washroom this time." She hated it when many families used the same sink and toilet and shower.

She had heard *Papá* say on the way up to Washington that the apple crop was small this year because of heavy frost in the spring. Many of their friends weren't coming this far north. Cousin Elena and her family were here, though, and were staying in another camp down near the river. Rosa wondered if she could go to visit her cousin sometime. Elena was just a year younger than she was. But *Mamá* and *Papá* had both warned her to avoid the river, so she probably couldn't play with Elena.

"Guess what we found!" Graciela's brown eyes sparkled. She jumped up and down with excitement.

"What did you find?"

"Somebody put up a slide and a swing for the kids, and there's a sandbox, and a big dog came to play with us, and. . . ."

"Slow down. You're telling me so many things at once that I can't understand you."

"The best thing is the dog," said Graciela. "He's brown and yellow, and he likes us."

"He probably belongs to the owner," said Rosa. "They must be good people to fix a playground for us."

"Push me," Juan said, as he climbed up on the seat of the swing.

"I'll give you one push; then we have to go to the cabin and eat. Maybe we can come back after supper. Hang on tight!" Rosa watched Juan's chubby legs trying to pump the swing. His black hair stood on end each time he swished forward.

Graciela pulled Rosa toward the sandbox. She showed her big sister the shovel and bucket in the sandpile. Sitting on a board in one corner of the sandbox, she piled the sand into a heap and started to make a sand house. Then, leaving the sandbox, with her black braids tucked behind her ears, Graciela climbed the steps to the top of the slide and slid down the short length.

Just then a big dog came bounding around the corner and went right to Rosa. His plumed tail moved back and forth.

"Oh, you're beautiful," Rosa said. "What's your name? Is it Goldie? Lassie? Pancho?" She patted the dog's soft brown and gold fur. "We'll have to find out more about you."

"*Niños*, come children. Come for supper."

"Oh, oh, *Mamá's* calling us. We better go." Rosa grabbed the hands of her younger sister and brother. The children ran back to their cabin with the dog following close behind.

"Go home, girl," Rosa said. "Find your master. We have to eat now." The dog cocked her head as if she understood. Her ears perked up, but she didn't move.

"Come and eat," *Papá* said. Rosa looked at her father as he stood in the doorway. She thought how handsome he was with his dark hair slicked down after being washed in the shower. His brown skin glistened, and his black mustache twitched when he smiled.

"*Papá! Papá!*" Juan jumped into his father's arms. Graciela grabbed *Papá's* legs. Rosa gave *Papá* a quick hug and then went to help *Mamá* fill the tortillas.

"What have my *niños* been doing today?" *Papá* asked.

"Oh, *Papá*," Graciela said. "There's a slide here, and a sandbox, and a swing, and a dog to play with."

"You won't have much time to play here at the house from now on. You must go with *Mamá* to the orchard tomorrow while she picks apples. You can play between the rows of trees." He looked at Rosa. "And my Rosita will be in school *mañana*."

"Tomorrow? Oh, *Papá*," said Rosa, "I don't want to go to school. Can't I help in the orchards?"

"No, the law says that children old enough to go to school can't work during school hours."

"Will you take me to school, if I have to go?"

"No, I can't go with you. I'll be in the orchard before you're awake. And *Mamá* will be there, too, with Juan and Graciela." He patted her shoulder. "I found out what time the bus comes. You just stand out by the road and the driver will pick you up at seven-thirty."

"But *Papá*, I don't know anybody. I won't know where to go when I get to school. Please let me stay home."

"No, Rosa. You must go to school. It's the law." He sat at the table on the one wooden chair. The children stood while *Mamá* served the tortillas. After *Papá* filled his tortilla with tomatoes and peppers and beans, Rosa and Graciela filled theirs. They carefully tucked the ends of the tortilla around the filling before they went to sit on the bed. *Mamá* helped Juan.

Sitting on the side of the mattress, Rosa tried to eat, but the food didn't taste good. All she could think about was going to school. How many schools had she been in? She remembered starting first grade in Mexico six years ago. Before that she had gone to Head Start for two months when they went to California during picking season. In the years since then she had been in probably twenty different schools, a few months at a time. She was always "the new girl," always the one they stared at, the one who had to leave the room to go for special help.

In one school last year, a boy named Jim had made fun of the way she talked. "What ees thees?" he had mimicked. Just thinking about it, a year later, made Rosa's face turn red.

"*Buena comida,* Maria," *Papá* said after he finished eating. "Good food."

"Rosa fixed the tortillas," *Mamá* said. "She's a good helper."

Rosa tried to smile when she heard the kind words. But not even a compliment could cheer her. She was worrying about going to school—*mañana*.

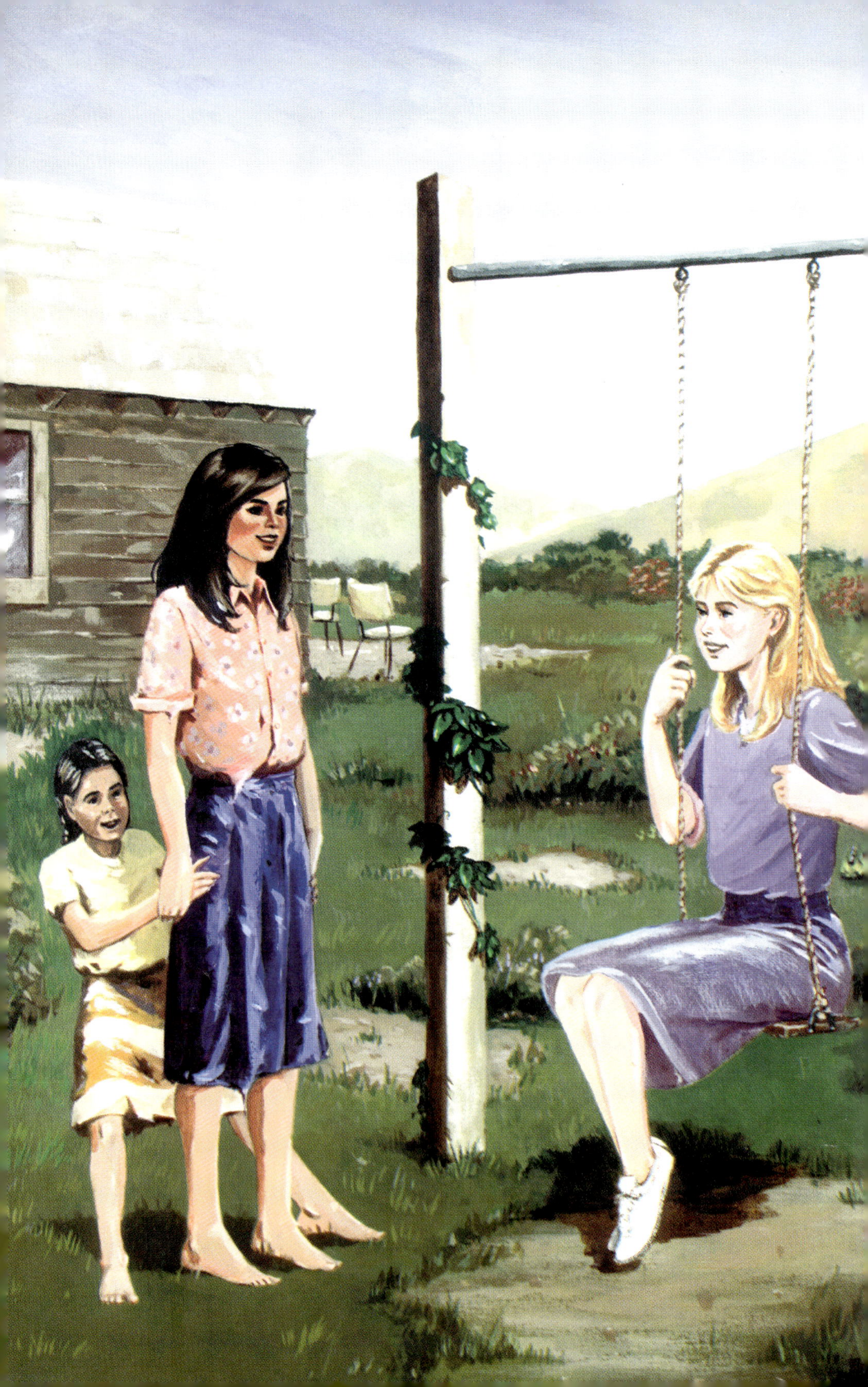

Chapter Two

A NEW FRIEND

"*Mamá,* can we go back and play some more?" Graciela pleaded after supper.

"Rosa can take you for a while. Then she has to take a shower so she is ready for school tomorrow."

Rosa knew it was useless to say anything more about school. Feeling more discouraged than ever, she took Juan by the hand and headed out the door of the cabin. Graciela followed.

The big dog met them outside the door. As soon as they started, he came behind, wagging his tail furiously.

Rosa reached to pat his long nose. "Lucky dog; you don't have to go to school."

Graciela ran ahead. Rosa saw her stop suddenly. "Rosa, Rosa, come quick," she called. "There's somebody here."

When Rosa rounded the corner of the last cabin, she saw a girl sitting in the swing. The girl was about her size, tall and thin, with long, blond hair. For a minute they stared at each other. Then the girl spoke.

"Hi, what's your name?"

"I'm Rosa Gomez."

"I'm Betty Baker," the girl said. "I see you've met Lady already."

"Is that her name?" Rosa said. "She followed us to the cabin. Whose dog is she?"

"She belongs to Mr. Jones. He owns the orchard here. My Dad came out to see him tonight; that's why I'm here. Daddy is a pastor, and the Joneses go to our church. Where do you live?"

"We live in one of the cabins. *Papá* is helping to pick apples."

"Have you started to school?" Betty asked.

"No, we just got here yesterday."

"Maybe you could come to my school," Betty said. "It's a Christian school and we have it in our church."

"School in a church?" Rosa asked. "How is that?"

"It's great," Betty said. "We study all the regular school subjects, plus we study the Bible. We have lots of fun."

Rosa began to feel a longing inside, half fear and half pleasure. She looked at Betty. "Does it cost money to go?"

"Yes, there's tuition. But I could ask Daddy about a scholarship for you. I know some of the kids get them if they can't afford to pay."

"I don't know if *Papá* would let me go." Rosa remembered that the school bus was coming in the morning. "How would I get to school?" she asked.

"Oh, that's simple," Betty said. "We could come and get you in our van. We pick up a couple of other students every day."

Rosa looked off to the hills surrounding the valley. The golden sun hung low in the west, and not a leaf moved on the apple trees. It was so still that she wondered if Betty could hear her heart beating wildly. Even Juan and Graciela were quiet.

It would be wonderful to have a friend like Betty, someone to talk to at recess, someone to eat lunch with at noon. Then another question entered her mind.

"I don't have nice clothes to wear." She noticed that Betty was wearing a shirt and jean skirt, but this was play time. She probably had beautiful clothes the rest of the time.

Betty chuckled. "You are a worrywart, aren't you?" She came over and stood close to Rosa. "They don't care what we wear as long as it's neat and clean. And modest," she added. "That skirt and blouse you have on is fine."

Betty grabbed Rosa's hand. "Come on; let's go ask my dad to talk to your dad and see if he'll let you go."

Rosa stood in the clean sunlight. "I don't think *Papá* will permit me, but we could perhaps ask."

"I love the way you talk," Betty said. "Maybe you could teach me to speak Spanish."

"Do you really mean that?" Rosa was amazed to think that someone would want to learn her language. "I would be very happy to help you learn Spanish," she said.

"Let's go see my dad now." Betty pulled her toward the path.

"I'll have to take Juan and Graciela back to *Mamá*."

"Oh, just bring them along. The big house is just down the road a ways."

"What if *Mamá* would call us."

"She won't. Don't worry; we'll just be a few minutes."

As long as she lived, Rosa would remember the feeling that sprang into her heart as she realized that she had found a friend, the first one she had ever had. Even if *Mamá* and *Papá* said no about the school, she would never forget Betty.

The four children bounded down the path which led to the house where the Joneses lived. Long spears of pink and orange light filtered between the trees in the late afternoon sunlight. The mist of fear cleared from Rosa's mind. She looked at Betty. Maybe she could share things with this new friend that she had never shared with anyone. From the orchard came the song of a robin, trilling and chortling, rising to join the song in her heart.

"You have to watch out for snakes sometimes when you walk through the orchard," Betty said. "The rattlers come down from the hills to get irrigation water in the orchard when it's as dry as it is now."

Rosa grabbed hold of Juan's and Graciela's hands and kept them close to her side when she heard that. Betty laughed. "I didn't mean to scare you. I just wanted you to know that there can sometimes be snakes in this area. I've got a four-year-old brother who can be a brat. I have to keep an eye on him, too." Just then they came close to the house. Lady, who had been following, charged ahead and raced toward two men who stood outside the house talking. One was tall and thin, the other older and heavier.

"There's my dad now," Betty said. "I'll tell him about you and ask him if he can come with us to where you live and talk to your parents."

Betty went to the younger man. He put his arm around her shoulder and looked at the other three children coming toward him. "Daddy, this is Rosa and her brother and sister," Betty said. "Can you come and talk to her dad about her coming to our school?"

Rosa made circles in the grass with her toe as she stood with her head down, hardly daring to look up at the two men. She felt Juan's hot, sweaty hand holding tight. Graciela stood beside her.

"Well, Betty, let's introduce your friends to Mr. Jones, too," Betty's dad said.

"I'm sorry, Mr. Jones," Betty said. "This is Rosa. Her daddy works for you, and they live in one of your cabins."

Mr. Jones smiled. "You must be the Gomez children. I'm happy to meet you. Your father is a good worker."

Rosa looked up. Mr. Jones liked *Papá*. And Mr. Jones must be the one who had fixed the play area for the workers' children. He is a good man, she decided.

"I see you've met Lady," he said. "She loves kids." He bent down to Juan. "And what is your name, young man?"

Juan hid his face in Rosa's skirt. "This is Juan," Rosa said. "And Graciela," she said, as she pulled her sister out from behind her.

Betty was impatiently pacing around her father. "Can we go ask Rosa's daddy if she can go to our school?"

"I suppose I can drop by there later. Let me finish talking to Mr. Jones; then I'll come over. Which cabin?"

"They're in the first one you come to," Mr. Jones said. "Lady, you stay here now. You've gallivanted long enough." He called the friendly dog to his side.

"We better get back," Rosa said. "*Mamá* will wonder where we are."

"All right, I'll see you later," Mr. Baker said.

Betty led the little group back down the path toward the cabins. Rosa followed, still holding Juan's hand. Lady pranced along beside them, ignoring her master's command.

"I'm scared," Rosa said. "I don't think *Papá* will let me go to your school."

"Let's pray and ask Jesus to help him," Betty said. "This is a good place right here." She stopped and took Rosa's hand in one of her hands and Graciela's hand in the other.

Rosa was puzzled. "You mean we could pray about something like that? Out here in the orchard?" She had prayed once in church, one of the few times that they had gone. She remembered the light coming through stained-glass windows, and how it made blue and red and yellow streaks over the people sitting in front of her. She remembered her prayer. She had asked God to give her a friend. But she never had stayed long enough anywhere to have a friend.

"Of course we can pray here," Betty said. "We pray at home and at school and at church, and wherever we are. Just close your eyes. I'll pray."

Rosa closed her eyes. She hoped Betty would pray quickly. If *Papá* came looking for them at the playground and they were gone, he'd be angry. And *Mamá* would scold.

"Dear God," Betty prayed. "Please help Rosa's father to let her come to my school. In Jesus' name I ask it, Amen."

Betty let go of Rosa's hand. "There, that's done. God will take care of it. Now let's go. I want to see where you live."

When the children came within sight of the cabin, Rosa was relieved to see that no one was out looking for them. Juan and Graciela went inside. Rosa motioned for Betty to come in. *Papá* had the radio on and was listening to the news on the station that broadcast in Spanish.

Mamá was nowhere in sight. "*Papá,* this is Betty," Rosa said. "Where is *Mamá?*"

"*Hola*, Betty, hello," said *Papá* as he turned down the volume on the radio. He turned to Rosa. "Your *mamá* went to the washroom to get a bucket of water for doing the dishes."

"What fun," Betty said. "It's sort of like camping, isn't it?" She looked around the cabin. "Where do you sleep, Rosa?"

"Graciela and Juan and I sleep on the floor," Rosa said.

"Isn't that hard?" Betty asked.

"It's not too bad. We have quilts under us. *Mamá* and *Papá* sleep on the bed."

Betty read the name on the stove. "Midget. What a cute little stove," she said. "Do you cook everything on this?"

"Yes," Rosa said. "I made tortillas on top of the stove this afternoon. And *Mamá* cooked the tomatoes and peppers and beans on it, too."

"How did you learn to make tortillas?"

Rosa smiled. What a silly question, she thought. "I've made tortillas since I was a little girl. I just watch how *Mamá* does it. A person can learn anything if he wants to."

"You're lucky. You get to cook," Betty said. "My mother lets me bake cookies sometimes, but that's about all."

Then the door opened and *Mamá* walked inside, carrying a full bucket of hot water. She looked startled when she saw Betty. Rosa saw the puzzled look in *Mamá's* eyes and quickly explained. "This is Betty. Her *papá* is a minister and he wants to talk to you and *Papá* about my going to their school."

"I hope you'll say yes when my daddy asks," Betty said. "Rosa is my friend now, and I want her to come to my school."

"Where is your school?" *Papá* said. "Isn't it the same one that Rosa will go to?"

"It's in our church," Betty said. "It's a Christian school."

"In the church?"

"Well, we use the Sunday school rooms for school classes during the week. Then on Sunday we have Sunday school classes in them."

Rosa looked at *Papá*. She couldn't tell if he was angry or pleased. Betty didn't seem to be afraid to talk to *Papá*. She rattled on as if she had known him all her life.

Suddenly there was a knock at the door. *Papá* went to answer. Betty's father stood at the door. He stuck out his hand to Mr. Gomez. "Hello, I'm Pastor Baker. I see you've met my daughter."

"Come in," *Papá* said. *"Buenas noches."*

"Good evening," Mr. Baker said. "Betty tells me that your daughter is interested in attending our school." He glanced at Betty. "Or maybe it's my daughter who wants her to come."

Papá hesitated. "I just heard about it. I need to know more about this school. Sit down, please." He pulled out one of the chairs for the pastor.

Betty stood next to Rosa and whispered, "Pray."

Mr. Baker cleared his throat. "We believe that the Bible is the Word of God and that all truth is God's truth. So we base our teaching on the words and truths in the Bible. In our school we have smaller classes than the public school. This way the teachers can work more closely with the children."

Papá was quiet. He seemed to be thinking. Finally he spoke: "Do you teach reading and arithmetic?"

"Oh yes," Mr. Baker said. "We teach the usual school subjects, along with the Bible. The advantage of a Christian school is that we put God first in all that we do."

"Does it cost anything for all this? We don't have much money."

"Yes," the pastor said. "Most of the parents pay. But we do have scholarships for those who can't afford the tuition."

Betty was having trouble keeping still. "Please let Rosa come," she pleaded. "She's my friend now. I'll help her with her English, and she's going to help me to learn Spanish."

Rosa's eyes lit up. Surely *Papá* would be happy about that. But Mr. Gomez was not convinced. "Who pays for these scholarships?" he said.

"Some of them are paid for by Christian people who have a real concern for children. Some money is raised through fundraisers put on by the school."

Rosa hardly dared to breathe through all the discussion. Would *Papá* let her go to school with Betty? She looked at her mother. *Mamá* was letting *Papá* do all the talking. She sat on the side of the bed holding Juan on her lap. Rosa wished that *Mamá* would speak up and tell *Papá* how much she wanted to have a friend. She wondered if it would help if she prayed right now. Betty said you could pray anywhere for anything.

She didn't know how to start. Betty had prayed, "Dear God, please help Rosa's father to let her come to my school." So Rosa prayed silently, "Dear God, please help *Papá* to let me go to Betty's school."

Papá stood up. He looked at Rosa. "Do you want to go to this Christian school?" His voice sounded gruff.

"Yes, *Papá*." Rosa took a deep breath. "I would like to go with my friend, Betty."

"How far away is the school?" asked *Papá*. "Could she walk?"

"We could pick her up, couldn't we, Daddy?" Betty said.

"Yes, if her parents will allow her to come, we'll see that she has transportation."

"All right," *Papá* said. "If she wants to go, and there is a ride, and if it doesn't cost anything, she can go."

Betty grabbed Rosa and swung her around the room. "Rosa, you're coming to school with me tomorrow."

"*Mañana*," Rosa said.

"*Mañana*," Betty echoed. "That means tomorrow, doesn't it?" Once again she waltzed Rosa around the room. Rosa looked out the window. The sky was alive with color. Red, yellow, orange, pink, purple, and blue blended together, filling the window. It splashed across the room, sending rays of color across the younger children and *Mamá*, and all over the bed. Rosa thought of the stained glass window in the church long ago and remembered her feeble prayer then, and the one she prayed now. Maybe there really is a God Who listens to children. For some reason *Papá* had agreed to her going to Betty's school. Was it an answer to Betty's prayer? Or hers? Either way it was a miracle.

"We'd better get home, Betty," Mr. Baker said. "Your mother will wonder what happened to us."

Betty gave Rosa a big hug. "I'll see you *mañana*. What's the Spanish word for friend?"

"*Amiga*."

"*Adiós, amiga*," said Betty.

"*Adiós, amiga,*" Rosa replied.

Betty and her father left. "Thank you, *Papá,*" Rosa said. "Thank you for letting me go to Betty's school." She felt the water in the bucket. "This is cold. I'll go and get another bucket and help with the dishes."

Quickly she filled the bucket from the faucet in the washroom, being careful not to spill any of the hot water. She had better hurry and get the dishes done so she could take a shower. She needed to wash her skirt and blouse, too, so they would be ready to wear to school.

On the way back to the cabin, Rosa saw the last soft pink and purple streaks fading in the sky. Dark shadows were forming on the surrounding hills, but spears of light touched the tops with golden fingers. It looked as if giant hands had molded the hills, leaving fingerprints up and down where they worked the clay. "The hand of God moves over all the earth." Somewhere she had heard that phrase. Could it be that the God Who made the world and everything in it cared for her? Did He know about a little Mexican girl who was afraid to go to school by herself? Was it too much to hope that He, too, could someday be her friend?

Chapter Three

THE CHRISTIAN SCHOOL

A loud roaring sound woke Rosa. She looked around. The curtain separating *Mamá* and *Papá's* bed from the rest of the room was pulled back to the wall. *Papá* and *Mamá* were gone. Graciela and Juan still slept. Where was *Mamá?* Rosa looked out the window. Rain. Why did it have to rain the first day of school?

Rosa poked Graciela. "Wake up, sleepyhead. Today I am going to school."

Graciela rolled over and pushed her tangled black hair out of her eyes. "Is it morning already? Where is *Mamá?* What's that loud noise?"

"I don't know." Rosa put her feet out from under the quilt and touched the wooden floor. She jerked back. "That floor is cold! Where are my sandals?" Rummaging around with her hands, she finally felt them under an edge of the quilt. She slid one, then the other, onto her bare feet, pulled her flannel nightgown over her head, and put on her blouse and skirt. "I'm going to the washroom," she said. "I'll see if *Mamá* is in there."

The warmth from the stove was beginning to take the chill off the room. If it was this cold in September, Rosa wondered, how would it be in winter?

Rosa opened the door. The roaring was louder. It sounded like an airplane landing nearby. What could it be? Through the soft rain she saw something in the orchard that looked like a windmill with its blades twirling. She covered her ears and ran for the washroom.

Mamá was inside. "Oh, I was just coming to wake you up," she said. "*Papá* had to leave early. He only had time to eat a cold tortilla before he had to leave for the orchard. He let me wait awhile before going to work, since it's raining."

What is that awful roaring sound, *Mamá?*" Rosa asked. "Is it that windmill thing in the orchard?"

"Yes," *Mamá* said. "It's called a wind machine. In the spring when the air on the ground is cold, it mixes up the air and brings warmer air down to the tiny apples to keep them from freezing. In the fall the owners sometimes use it to help dry the trees so the workers can pick apples when it rains. Since it rained last night, Mr. Jones must have had it turned on so the pickers wouldn't get soaked this morning. He's a kind man."

Rosa hurried back to the cabin with *Mamá* close behind her. Graciela sat on the floor with a quilt wrapped around her shoulders. "What is that awful noise, *Mamá?*"

Mamá explained the wind machine again as she put another chunk of wood in the stove. Soon the tortillas were warming. While Juan slept, *Mamá* and the girls ate tortillas with leftover beans. *Mamá* drank coffee, and the girls had hot chocolate.

After breakfast Rosa paced back and forth. "I wonder if Mr. Baker and Betty will remember to pick me up?" She visited the washroom again to look in the mirror and see how her hair looked. Smoothing down a few loose strands, she noticed how black it was and how brown her face was. *Will they make fun of the way I look and talk?*

Dodging puddles in the muddy path, she headed back to the cabin. "*Mamá,* do I look all right?" Rosa straightened her skirt and tucked her blouse inside the elastic waistband.

"You look pretty, my Rosita," *Mamá* said. "Be a good girl and learn much."

"Where will you be when I get home?"

"I'll probably be in the south orchard, picking goldens," *Mamá* said. "You come and find us after school and help watch the little ones."

"They're here!" Graciela shouted as she looked out the window. "I see the van. Betty's getting out."

Rosa opened the door just as Betty came running to the cabin. "*Hola,*" she said, as she pushed back her wet hair. "See, I'm already learning Spanish."

"*Hola,*" Rosa responded with a smile. "I'm ready to go."

Waving goodbye to *Mamá* and Graciela, the two girls hurried toward the van.

"Good morning, Rosa," said Mr. Baker.

"Good morning," Rosa said. She quickly sat beside Betty and buckled the seat belt. Two boys sat in the seat behind her.

This is Rosa Gomez," Betty said. "And that's Bill Barnes and my brother, Jerry, in back. They're both in seventh grade."

Rosa turned around and saw a blond boy who looked like Betty. *That must be Jerry.* The other boy was shorter and darker. "Hello," she said in a quiet voice. She felt like hiding somewhere.

"Hi," the boys said.

"Don't look so scared," Jerry said. "We won't bite you."

When the van arrived at the church, Rosa noticed that the rain had stopped. She followed Betty into the building.

"Let's go into the office first," Betty said. "My dad told them you were coming, but you'll need to fill out some forms to register."

After filling out the forms with Betty's help, Rosa followed her new friend to the sixth-grade classroom. The room smelled like wet sweaters and chalk dust. Twelve desks stood in rows. In the windows, geraniums bloomed. A lady was writing an assignment on the chalkboard. "Mrs. Jenson, this is Rosa Gomez," Betty said.

The teacher turned around with a smile. "Good morning, Rosa. I'm so happy you're here. Pastor

Baker called last night and told me I had a new pupil coming." She walked toward the window. "Here is your desk. I'm glad that you can speak Spanish. Perhaps you can teach us." She turned to Betty, "Betty, will you show Rosa where the restroom is? I'll get her books ready."

Rosa knew she was going to like Mrs. Jenson. She was glad that Betty was in her room, too. It was almost too much to believe that she had a friend, and a teacher who was glad to have her in her room.

They were nearly to the door of the girls' restroom when a tall, redheaded boy stopped them. "What do we have here? A Mexican?" He pretended he was sniffing the air. "Do I smell tacos? Or is it refried beans?"

"Just ignore him," Betty said. Rosa wanted to dash into the restroom, but the boy blocked her way. "Hey, you're kind of cute," he said. "You've sure got a nice tan." He laughed.

Then Jerry, Betty's older brother, came down the hall. He saw the stormy look on Betty's face and Rosa's frightened expression. "What's going on?" he said.

"Bud's teasing Rosa," Betty said.

"Cut it out, Bud," Jerry said. "How would you like to be new here and have someone make fun of you?"

"Oh, I just wanted to get a rise out of your sister," Bud said. "I didn't mean anything."

Betty and Rosa took advantage of Jerry's help and ducked into the girls' room.

"I'm sorry this happened, Rosa," Betty said. "Though this is a Christian school, not everyone here acts like a Christian. That Bud thinks he's so smart! I'm glad Jerry came along when he did."

"It's all right, Betty," Rosa said. "Let's go back to our room." Her heart pounded as hard as it had the time that Jim had made fun of the way she talked, but she was determined to act as if nothing was wrong.

When they returned to the classroom, everyone was seated. Mrs. Jenson introduced Rosa to the class and opened her Bible. Rosa looked surprised. She had supposed that they would begin with assignments for the day.

"Today we are continuing our study of the life of Jesus," Mrs. Jenson said. "This is the story of Jesus when he was twelve years old." She held up beautiful pictures as she told the story. Then she read the account from Luke, chapter two, verses 41–52, as the children followed along in their Bibles. Betty reached over and shared hers with Rosa.

After their teacher finished reading the Scripture, the class discussed how Jesus had obeyed Joseph and Mary, even though He was the son of God. Then Mrs. Jenson prayed. She asked God to guide them in the rest of their studies that day. She prayed for Rosa and asked God to bless her and to help her to feel at home in their class. Rosa couldn't believe what she was hearing. Mrs. Jenson had actually prayed for her! She looked around to see if anyone else was shocked. All heads were bowed and eyes closed. No one seemed surprised.

When Mrs. Jenson finished praying, she announced that the school would be having a program the following week. "Our class will be singing and putting on a skit," she said. "If anyone would like to sing a solo or play an instrument, be sure to see me, and we'll work it into the program."

After the announcements, Mrs. Jenson asked Rosa to come to the teacher's desk. "Don't worry if you can't keep up in some assignments," she said. "I'll help you if you have any trouble, and Betty can help you catch up after school."

Rosa relaxed, knowing that she didn't have to do everything today. She wondered if she would be sent out of the room as she had been in so many schools. Mrs. Jenson didn't mention it.

The morning passed quickly with reading, math, and science. At noon she joined Betty and the rest of the class in the Fellowship Hall of the church. Tables were set up. Everyone but Rosa had brought a sack lunch. She had forgotten all about her lunch. "Don't worry," Betty said. "You can share my sandwich. I've got an extra apple and cookies." She poured milk into her thermos cup. "Here, you drink from the cup and I'll drink out of the thermos bottle."

Pastor Baker came into the room and asked the blessing on their food. Rosa bowed her head with the others. It sounded to her as if the pastor was talking to Jesus like he would talk to a friend. She wished she knew Jesus like that.

When she looked up, Rosa saw Bud sitting with some of his friends at the next table. She felt her face turning red. She didn't talk much to Betty, because she didn't want Bud to hear her poor English. She hoped he would leave her alone. Jerry walked by and gave her a big smile. Rosa's heart beat faster. She wondered if she would ever have the courage to talk to him.

"Rosa, I just had a neat idea," Betty said, interrupting Rosa's thoughts. "Why don't you sing at the program? You could sing a song in Spanish. You'd be the hit of the program."

"The hit?" Rosa questioned. "I don't understand."

"I mean, you would really be special. Would you do it?"

"Oh, no, I couldn't sing in front of people," Rosa said. "I like to sing, but not by myself in a program."

"Please, would you do it for me?" Betty begged. "Let's go tell Mrs. Jenson."

"I'd be so scared, Betty."

"Please! I'll help you find a song from our chorus book and you can sing it in Spanish. Would you, please?"

Rosa didn't know what to do. Her new friend had been so kind to her that she didn't want to disappoint her, but the very thought of singing in front of strangers frightened her. Yet, she wanted to please Betty. "I suppose I could try, if you'll help me," she said.

"Great! Let's go now and tell Mrs. Jenson. She should be back in the room by now." Betty jumped up. She picked up her empty sack and tossed it into the wastebasket. Then she grabbed the thermos bottle and put it in her book bag and pulled Rosa toward the door.

When they arrived in the room, Mrs. Jenson was sitting at her desk correcting papers. She looked up. "Hi, girls; what can I do for you?"

Betty spoke up. "Mrs. Jenson, I have the neatest idea for our program. Rosa's going to sing for us in Spanish."

Rosa ducked her head down and stared at the floor. She wished she were home right now in the safety of *Mamá's* arms. How had she gotten into something like this?

Mrs. Jenson looked at Rosa. "Would you like to do this, dear?"

Rosa couldn't risk losing her new friend or disappointing her teacher, so she said, "Yes, I'll do it, if Betty will help me find a song."

"Good," Betty squealed. "Let's go into the church right now and look in the chorus book." She linked her elbow with Rosa's arm and herded her off toward the sanctuary. "We've got about ten minutes before we have to get back to class. I know we can find something."

Inside the sanctuary Rosa paused. "Is this where you have church?"

"Yes," Betty said. "What church do you attend?"

"We don't go very often. Once when I was about eight we went to a big cathedral. I still remember the beautiful colors coming through the stained-glass windows."

"You mean you haven't gone to church since you were eight?" Betty's eyes got big. "Maybe you can come with me this Sunday."

"I'll ask *Papá*," said Rosa. She looked around at the pews with their bright orange pads and dark brown wooden backs. On the platform the pulpit stood like a lone sentry on duty. "This is different from the cathedral, but I like it."

"Here's our chorus book," Betty said. She flipped through the pages. "Here's an easy one. It's called 'I Have Decided to Follow Jesus.' "

"Will you help me learn it?"

"Sure, I'll help you. I can play the piano pretty well. My mother will help you, too. She's the music teacher for our school."

"What does your father do at the school?" Rosa asked. "I know he is pastor of the church, but I saw him this noon when we ate."

"He drives the van to pick up children and helps whenever he's needed at school. He likes to talk to the kids, so he usually comes in and prays before lunch and then eats with us."

"Where is your house?"

"Oh, we live about a mile and a half from the church, in the parsonage."

"What's a parsonage?" Rosa asked.

"That's the house owned by the church, where the pastor and his family live." Betty went to the piano and began playing the melody line of the song. "Come here and tell me what 'I Have Decided to Follow Jesus' would be in Spanish."

Rosa looked at the words. "In Spanish it would be *'He Decidido Seguir a Cristo,'*" she said.

Betty sang the chorus through in English, and then Rosa tried it in Spanish. "You have a beautiful voice," Betty said. "I'm really glad you're going to sing for the program."

"We better go back to our room, hadn't we?" Rosa asked.

Betty looked at her watch. "Wow! It is late! We better go."

The girls ran down the hall and into their room just as the teacher said, "Take out your spelling books, please."

Rosa's stomach did flip-flops. Spelling was hard for her. So many English words had special rules. She remembered the trouble she had last year learning the difference between *wait* and *weight*. They sounded the same but had different meanings and were spelled differently. Sometimes in English *c* sounded like *k;* other times it sounded like *s*. The *k* sometimes was silent. Confusing. Rosa thought she would never get it straight.

Spanish vowels were clear and precise sounds. In Spanish every letter sounded the same whenever you used it. Of course, some consonants had the same sound, like *b* and *v*. And some people had trouble rolling the *r*'s in Spanish. But to Rosa there was no comparison. Spanish was easier.

Mrs. Jenson remembered her new pupil. "Rosa, you haven't had a chance to study these words, so don't worry about today's lesson."

Thank goodness. Rosa was glad she could take the words home. She'd work hard to learn them all before the week was over.

At the end of the day, Rosa's head was spinning. So many new things to learn! She was glad that Betty was there to help her. The other girls were friendly, too. And Mrs. Jenson was the best teacher she had ever known. Rosa couldn't wait to get home to tell *Mamá* all about her first day at the Christian school.

At ten minutes to three, Mrs. Jenson said, "Rosa, could you tell us how to say 'We'll see you tomorrow' in Spanish?"

Rosa thought a minute. " '*Hasta mañana,*' means 'until tomorrow,' " she said.

"*Hasta mañana*," the class said in unison. It sounded good to Rosa. When the bell rang, she gathered up her notebook and books to take home. Betty waited for her. "I'll show you where we wait for the van," she said.

The girls went to the parking lot. The van was already there with Mr. Baker sitting in the driver's seat. "Hello, Rosa," he said. "Did you have a good day?"

"*Muy bien.* I mean, very good," she said.

"I'm glad to hear that. I've been praying for you today."

Rosa was surprised again to think that the pastor had prayed for her. "*Gracias,*" she said. "Thank you."

When they arrived at her cabin, Rosa jumped out with a smile. "*Adiós, amiga,*" Betty said. "*Hasta mañana.*"

"*Hasta mañana,*" said Rosa. She put her books in the cabin and headed for the orchard.

Running lightly between the rows of apple trees, she saw how shiny the leaves and apples looked after the rain. The apples were as big as softballs and as golden as the sunlight. She had heard *Papá* say that they were Golden Delicious. Rosa wondered if they could pick some to eat. She noticed that the ground was dry already. It didn't seem to rain very hard when it did rain in Washington State.

"*Mamá,* where are you?" she called. Finally she saw *Mamá* and *Papá* working at the end of a row. *Mamá* carried a canvas bag with straps over her shoulders. She was emptying it into a bin. She unloosed the bottom of the bag and carefully let the apples roll out into the large wooden bin. Then she buckled it again. *Papá* was on the fruit ladder.

The ladder with its one leg prop looked tall and dangerous, but *Papá* didn't seem to mind. He reached out and picked as fast as Rosa's eyes could follow, one hand twisting the apple off the branch, the other placing it in his picking bag.

Graciela and Juan played between the rows of trees. Graciela had made a pretend playhouse with sticks outlining each room. "Well, look at your house, little sister," Rosa said. "So many rooms." She picked up Juan and gave him a hug. "How is *mi hermano*, my brother, today?"

"Did you have a good time?" *Mamá* asked.

"Yes, *Mamá,* it was fun." Rosa smiled, remembering. She decided she wouldn't tell *Mamá* about Bud. "I have the nicest teacher, and they want me to sing in the program next week."

"Sing? My Rosita is going to sing at the school program?"

"Yes, *Mamá*. I was scared at first, but Betty and her mother will help me learn a song to sing in Spanish." She swung Juan around as she spoke. "Can you come to the program next Tuesday night?"

"I don't know," *Mamá* said. "We'll ask *Papá*."

That night as Rosa lay on the floor snuggled under her quilt, she thought about the chorus she would sing—"I Have Decided to Follow Jesus." She wondered what it meant to follow Jesus. Maybe she would find out soon. In her heart there was a longing for God.

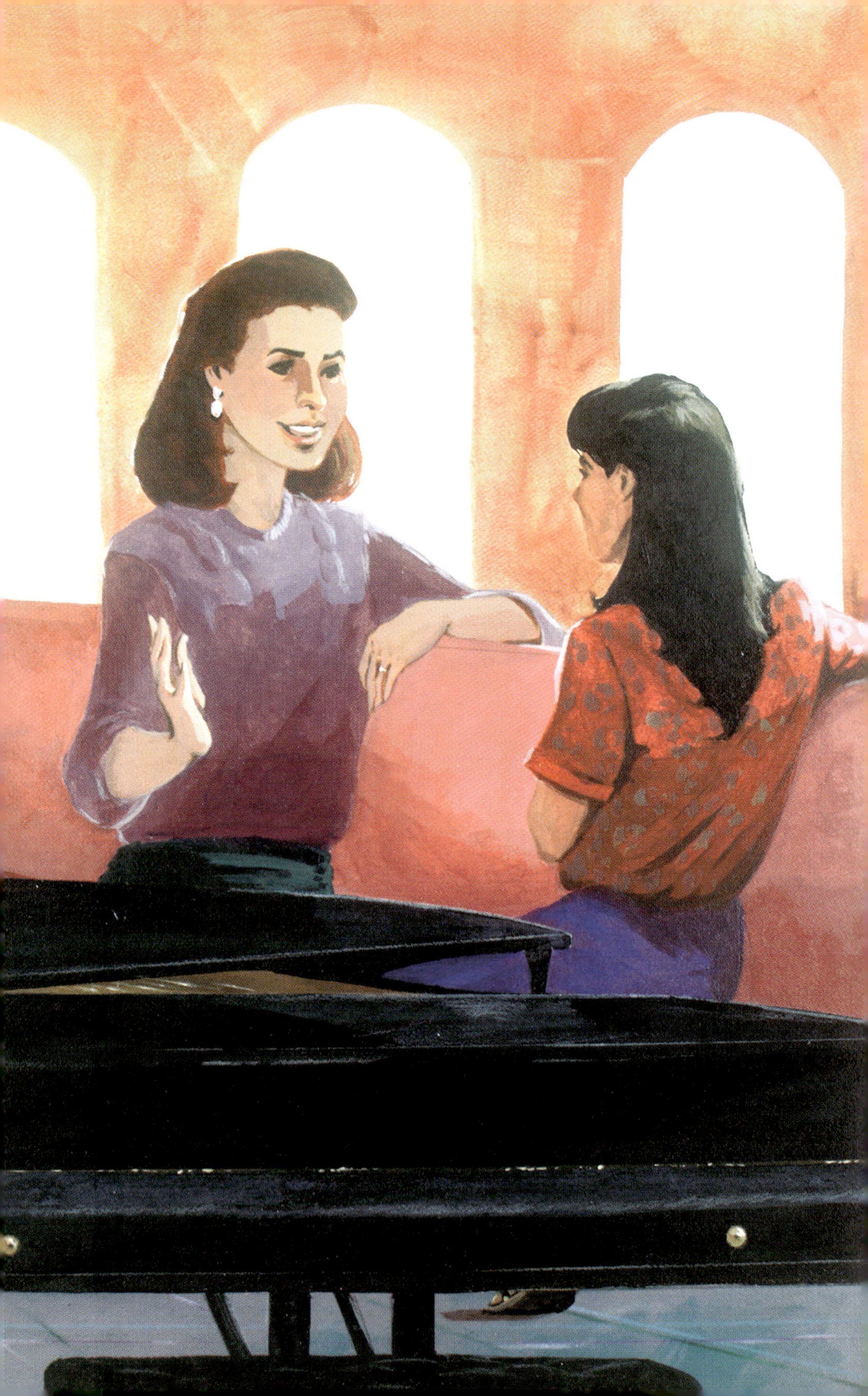

Chapter Four

THE PROGRAM

The week passed quickly. Each day, Rosa felt more at home in her new school. Each day, she learned new English words, and it became easier to read and do her work. Betty helped her as they rode to and from school in the van.

After lunch every day, Mrs. Baker helped Rosa with her song for the program. One day, Rosa asked about something that had been bothering her ever since she came to the Christian school.

"Mrs. Baker, what does it mean to follow Jesus?" Rosa was too shy to look straight at Mrs. Baker, so she kept her eyes on the chorus book. "It says here in the song, 'I have decided to follow Jesus. No turning back, no turning back.'"

"I'll be happy to tell you what it means," Betty's mother said. She got up from the piano bench and motioned for Rosa to sit beside her on the front pew. "Jesus is the Son of God. He left heaven and came as a tiny baby to live on earth." She looked carefully at Rosa. "Do you know the story of how He grew up, and how He died for our sins?"

"We learned in our class how He was left behind when He was twelve years old and how He obeyed His parents and lived with them until He grew up." Rosa remembered that story especially because her family often traveled in a group. She knew it would be easy to get lost with so many aunts and uncles and cousins together.

"Yes," Mrs. Baker continued. "He stayed with His mother and Joseph until the time came for Him to preach the good news of salvation. He healed the sick and even raised the dead. Then He died on the cross and took all the sin of the world upon Him there at Calvary. But He didn't stay dead. He rose again and is living today."

"Where does He live?" Rosa asked.

"That's the exciting part," Mrs. Baker said. "He will live in our heart if we ask Him in."

"Rosa, hurry, the bell's ringing." Betty burst into the sanctuary. "You'll be late for class. Oh, hi, Mom. How's Rosa doing with her song?"

"She's doing fine." Mrs. Baker spoke directly to Rosa. "Think about the things I was telling you. We'll talk about it again soon."

Rosa left the room with Betty. What strange things Betty's mother had said! To think that Jesus could live in your heart. How could that be?

The classroom buzzed with excitement. The program was tonight, and everyone was practicing. Some had Bible verses to say. Some were working on their parts for the play that they were performing. Still others had musical numbers to sing or play. Rosa felt nervous just thinking about her solo. She hoped no one would laugh when she sang in Spanish. She wondered if *Papá* and *Mamá* and the children would come to hear her sing. When she had asked *Papá* about it he had said, "We'll see."

The bell rang. On the way home, Betty told Rosa that they would pick her up at six-thirty since the program was at seven. All the children had to be there early.

"Is your family coming tonight?" Mr. Baker asked.

"I don't know yet," Rosa said. "I hope so."

"Mom said you do a great job singing," Jerry said. "Tell your parents they better come and hear you."

Rosa felt her face turning red. Why did she always blush when Jerry said anything to her? He was the nicest boy she had ever known. But she never knew what to say to him when he tried to talk to her. What was wrong?

When the van pulled in front of her cabin, she quickly jumped out and ran into the house. No one was there.

"*Mamá, Mamá,*" she called. No answer.

Rosa didn't know which orchard the pickers were in today so she decided to wait at the cabin. She took the chorus book and began to practice her song. "*He decidido seguir a Cristo. He decidido seguir a Cristo. He decidido seguir a Cristo. No vuelvo atrás. No vuelvo atrás.*" Then she sang it in English. "I have decided to follow Jesus. I have decided to follow Jesus. I have decided to follow Jesus. No turning back, no turning back."

As she sang, Rosa thought about what Mrs. Baker had said about Jesus. What a wonderful thing that He did, dying on the cross to forgive the sins of the world. It was incredible to think that He died for her sins. I want to follow Jesus, she decided. But I still don't know what to do to get my sins forgiven so I can follow Him. Maybe I can ask Mrs. Baker sometime. If Betty hadn't come in saying the bell rang I might have found out today.

"What am I going to wear tonight?" Rosa muttered. She went to the wall behind the bed and took all her clothes off the hook. There was the blue cotton skirt that she wore nearly every day and the faded pink blouse that she wore with it. She laid them out on the bed and compared them with the black skirt and red blouse that she had on today. The skirt she was wearing wasn't quite as worn. A pair of ragged jeans and a flannel shirt were all that was left on the hook.

Then there was the yellow dress that Betty had given her yesterday. It still hung on the hanger on which Betty had brought it. Betty had said the dress was too short for her, and could Rosa use it? Rosa knew that the real fact was that Betty was probably tired of always seeing Rosa wear the same two skirts and blouses. She didn't know what Jerry would think of her wearing his sister's dress. Oh, well, what did it matter what Jerry thought about her, anyway?

Rosa looked out the window. It was starting to get dark. She should get supper started, or they wouldn't get to the program on time. She hung her clothes on the hook again and left the yellow dress on the bed. It stood out like a bright patch of sunlight on the brown quilt.

After her parents came in with the younger children and supper was finished, Rosa went behind the sheet and put on the beautiful yellow dress. She walked out, feeling self-conscious. "Pretty, pretty," Graciela said. Juan echoed her, followed by *Mamá,* saying how pretty she was.

"You look nice," *Papá* said.

"Can you come to hear me sing?" Rosa asked one last time.

"We'll see," *Papá* said. "I hear the van stopping out front. You better hurry so you don't miss your ride."

Rosa was relieved to see that it was just Betty and her little brother Timmy with Mrs. Baker in the van. She wondered where Jerry was. Betty answered her unspoken question.

"Jerry walked over to the church with Daddy earlier. They're setting up the microphones and getting the platform ready."

When they got to the church, Rosa saw that the parking lot was nearly filled. Her stomach started doing flip-flops. She couldn't believe that she was actually going to sing a solo in front of so many people.

Jerry stood at the door giving out programs. "You look nice tonight," he said.

"*Gracias*," Rosa said softly in Spanish. She was too nervous to remember the English word for thank you.

Betty led her to the section where the sixth graders were to sit. "Let's leave our stuff here and go see who's here," she said. "I sure hope Bud doesn't show up."

Rosa had forgotten the possibility of Bud's being at the program. She couldn't sing in front of him. "Do you really think he'll come?"

"Oh, he probably will. All the seventh graders are supposed to help usher. That's why Jerry is at the door."

The church was nearly filled, and it was only six forty-five. Parents sat in the middle and back sections. Younger brothers and sisters squirmed beside them. Rosa looked from the front to the back to see if her family was there. They weren't.

Betty's brother Timmy got away from his mother and followed Betty and Rosa down the aisle. When Betty told him to go back, he ignored her. "If you can walk around, I can," he said.

"I'm gonna tell Dad on you," Betty said. "You get back to your seat."

Just then Mrs. Baker began to play the piano. Timmy heard the music and scurried back to the front pew nearest the piano. Betty and Rosa turned and went back to their places with the other sixth graders.

The first number on the program was a welcome by the kindergarten class. That was followed by a play put on by the first and second grades. The other classes followed. Rosa began to twist her long hair in her hands. She had never been so frightened in her life. Why had she agreed to sing? When the fifth grade had finished with their music and Scriptures, she was a wreck.

"Rosa Gomez will now sing a song in Spanish." Rosa heard the announcement, but she couldn't make herself go up on the platform.

"It's your turn," Betty said, as she gave Rosa a little push. "Go on. I'll be praying for you."

In a daze Rosa walked up to the platform. She looked out at the audience. The church was full. It's hot in here, she thought. She noticed that the doors were open. In the doorway was a man who looked like her father. Behind him stood a dark-haired lady with two little children beside her. Could it be? Yes, it was *Papá* and *Mamá*. They came! They came to hear their Rosa sing!

Mrs. Baker played the introduction on the piano. Rosa lifted her head and began to sing in a clear, strong voice, "*He decidido seguir a Cristo. He decidido seguir a Cristo.*" She had just started the third phrase when she heard a tittering beginning in the back of the church. Rosa's heart pounded furiously. Why were they laughing at her? The snickering spread from the back of the church to the front. Even Timmy was laughing.

Rosa felt her face getting red, but she kept singing. "*He decidido seguir a Cristo. No vuelvo atrás, no vuelvo atrás.*" She couldn't turn back now. Betty was praying for her, and *Papá* and *Mamá* had come to hear her sing. Even if they all laughed at her, she would keep singing. She would do it for her parents and for Betty and for her teacher and maybe even for Jesus. She knew then that she wanted to follow Jesus, even if people did make fun of her. She wanted to be a Christian.

The song finally ended, and Rosa walked off the platform. She couldn't believe her ears. Everyone was clapping for her, and the applause went on and on. She slipped into her seat as Betty whispered to her, "You did great. Just great."

"But they laughed at me," Rosa whispered. She was almost in tears.

"You silly thing," Betty whispered back. "They weren't laughing at you. The doors were open and a cat walked in. It came up the aisle, and when it walked past, people laughed. They were laughing at the cat, not you."

What a relief! They weren't laughing because she was a Mexican, or because she sang in Spanish. And they had clapped as if they really enjoyed the song. Rosa enjoyed the rest of the program. She couldn't wait to get back to see *Papá* and *Mamá*. She wondered what they thought about their daughter singing in front of these people.

After the benediction, Rosa slipped out the side door so she could get back to where *Papá* and *Mamá* were before they left. As she hurried through the darkness, she almost ran into Bud. "Hey, where you going so fast, little Mex?" he said.

Rosa tried to ignore him, but he stood in front of her, blocking her way. "How'd you like the kitty cat I sent down to see you while you were singing?"

Rosa was furious. "Did you do that?"

Bud laughed. "Funniest thing I ever saw. People laughing while you sang. Your face was so red I thought you'd explode."

"It wasn't funny." Rosa tried to think of the right words to say in English. "It was a mean trick," she finally blurted out. "Now get out of my way, please."

"What's your rush? You look mighty cute tonight in that yellow dress. Why don't we take a little walk and get better acquainted?" Bud grabbed Rosa's hand.

"Let me go. Let me go. Help!" Rosa yelled.

"What's going on?" Jerry had been standing just inside the door and came outside when he heard Rosa's cry. He grabbed Bud by the shoulders and shoved him to one side. "Leave Rosa alone." As the boys scuffled, Rosa ran to the front of the church building. She saw the rusty van pulling out of the parking lot.

"*Papá, Papá*," she called. But they were already heading down the road. Tears came to her eyes. She wanted to ride home with *Papá* and *Mamá,* but they didn't know that. She headed back inside the church to look for Betty.

Betty was helping her mother straighten up the platform. "Where have you been?" she asked.

Rosa joined them on the platform. "My family came tonight. They really came. I tried to get back to see them before they left, but I missed them."

Mrs. Baker hugged Rosa. "I'm so happy that your parents came to hear you. You sang so nicely."

"She thought people were laughing at her," Betty said.

"I heard that laughing, too," Mrs. Baker said. "What was it about?"

"A cat got inside the church and walked up the aisle. It was kind of funny to see it marching up front to the music. As it went past, people started to laugh."

"The cat didn't just get in by himself," Rosa said.

"What do you mean?"

"I saw Bud outside and he told me he let the cat in on purpose while I was singing."

Betty snorted. "That creep! What a mean trick! Where is he? I'll tell him what I think of his sense of humor."

"Oh no!" Rosa remembered where she had left Bud. "Jerry was after him. We have to see if Jerry is all right."

The girls went out the side door. No one was there. "It looks like they're gone. I wonder where they went." Betty looked behind the shrubs that lined the church. They walked around the church and parking lot, but there was no sign of either boy.

Rosa felt terrible. What if Jerry was hurt because of her? She would never forgive herself.

They went back inside the church. "Have you seen Jerry?" Betty asked her mother.

"No; he was supposed to help us get the chairs off the platform, but I haven't seen him. Maybe he's outside talking to some of his friends."

"He's not outside," Betty said. "Rosa saw him fighting with Bud right after the program. Bud was trying to give Rosa a hard time."

Mrs. Baker gathered up her music and took Timmy by the hand. "You come with me, young man. I don't want to have two missing sons."

Then Betty's father came inside. "As soon as I get the lights turned off we'll leave," he said.

"Have you seen Jerry?" Mrs. Baker asked.

"He's in the van. He said he doesn't feel very well."

Rosa followed the Baker family to the school van. What an evening this had been! She wondered what to say to Jerry. *Should I thank him? Should I ask him if he is all right?*

Jerry was huddled in the back seat. "Are you okay?" his mother asked. Rosa was relieved that she didn't have to ask.

"Yeah, I guess."

"What happened, son?" Mr. Baker asked.

"Oh, I just got in a fight with Bud."

"You know better than to fight with the other boys."

Mrs. Baker interrupted. "Don't scold him. He'll explain what happened."

Nothing more was said about the fight.

Betty talked all the way home. "Did you hear them clap when you sang? You were brave to keep singing when you thought they were laughing at you. Can you believe that Bud did that to you?" Rosa wished that Betty would stop talking. She didn't feel very brave. She felt bad that Jerry got in trouble for fighting. And she wanted to be with her family more than anything else right now.

When the van stopped, Rosa thanked Mr. Baker for the ride. Then she glanced back in the darkness. "Thank you for your help," she whispered.

"That's okay," Jerry said.

Rosa jumped out of the van and ran to the cabin. *Mamá* met her at the door. "Oh, Rosa, you did a good job singing."

"Where is *Papá?*"

"He's in the washroom."

"Oh, *Mamá,*" Rosa said, "I'm so glad you came to the program tonight. I wanted you there so badly."

Rosa smiled. "When I saw *Papá* in the doorway I was so glad. It is so good to have family when you're scared." She laughed. "And I was scared." Rosa went into *Mamá's* arms. "Oh, *Mamá,* it's good to be home."

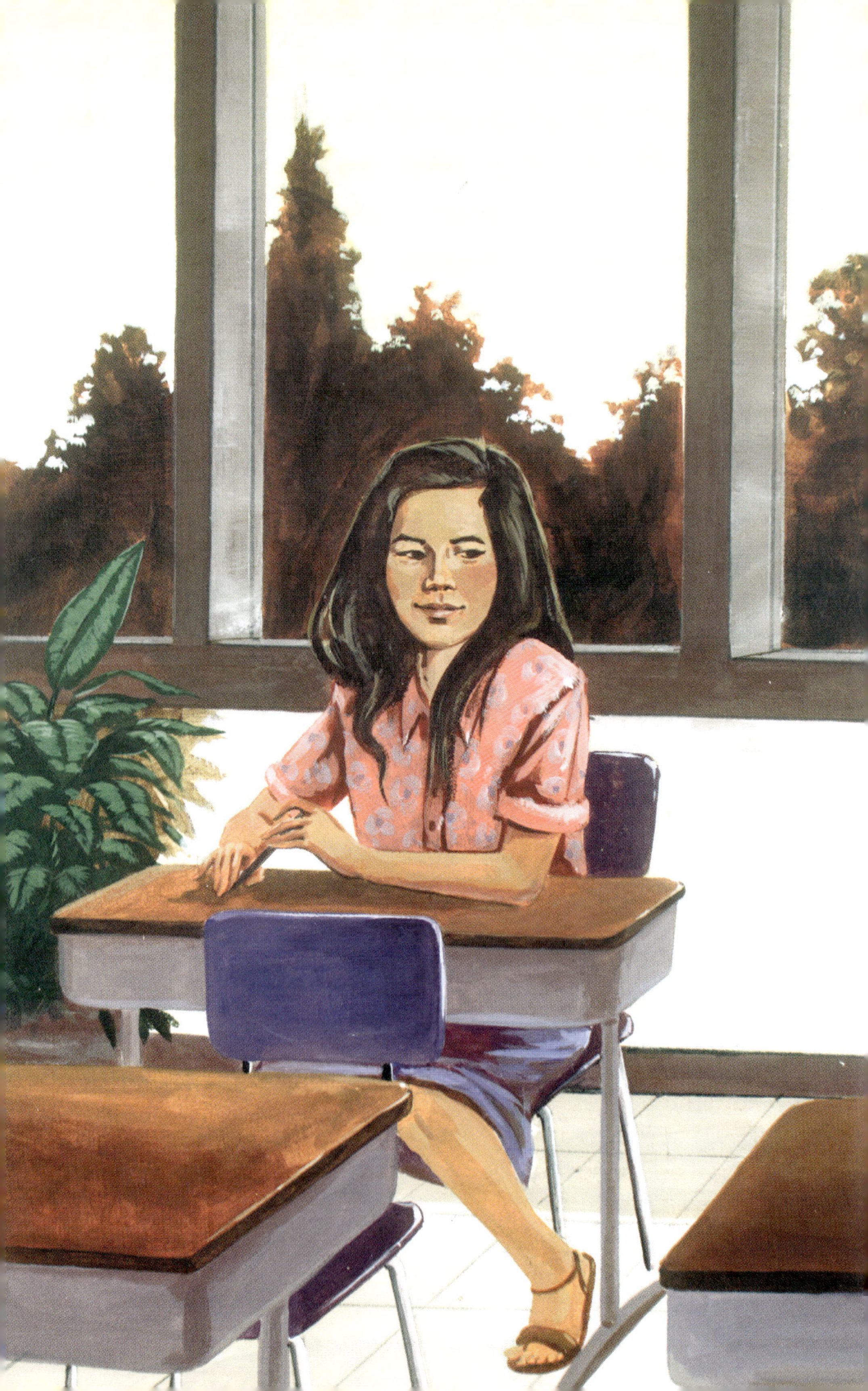

Chapter Five

THE RATTLESNAKE

The day after the program, the classroom was buzzing with excitement. Rosa overheard a conversation between Betty and another classmate. "Didn't Rosa do a good job singing?" Betty said to the girl. When the classmate agreed, saying it was the best thing on the program, Rosa felt like she would explode with joy.

Rosa felt good about everything today. She had seen Jerry at lunch, and he seemed all right. Her teacher had given her a hug and told her how well she had sung, and the best news was at breakfast when *Papá* had said they might stay in Washington State longer, maybe even until the end of the year. His boss, Mr. Jones, had mentioned the possibility of another job for *Papá* after the apple harvest ended. Rosa could hardly believe her ears. They never stayed in one place more than six or seven weeks. To think that they might stay through December was almost too much to hope for. She couldn't wait to get home to talk to *Mamá* about it.

When the school day ended, Betty called Rosa aside and asked if she could go on a picnic with her Saturday. "You could come home with me after school Friday and stay overnight at my house. We'll go down to the river and take our lunch and have a great time."

"I'm not supposed to go near the river," Rosa said. She wanted to go with Betty, but she knew *Mamá* and *Papá* would never give their permission. "My parents won't let me go."

"Couldn't you just ask if you could spend the weekend with your cousin Elena?"

"You mean lie to *Mamá* and *Papá?*" Rosa was shocked at the idea.

"Well, it wouldn't exactly be lying. You could come home with me after school, and we could go to Elena's and ask if she wants to come on the picnic with us. That way you would be at Elena's, even if it is only for a few minutes. Your parents wouldn't know the difference."

Rosa thought about it. It would be fun to be with Betty, and she'd get to see Jerry at the Bakers' house. Maybe it wouldn't be wrong. She made up her mind. "All right. I'll ask them tonight and then let you know tomorrow."

When Rosa got home, she found a note on the table. "Come to the south orchard and help take care of the little ones."

Rosa put her empty lunch sack on the table so it would be ready to fill the next morning. She changed into jeans and her old shirt and headed toward the orchard. Walking through the orchard at this time of year was fun. The pungent odor of apples filled the air. Warm September sunshine sifted through the trees and made shadows on the ground. The nights were cool now, but the days still felt like summer. Rosa remembered that *Papá* said the cool nights were necessary for the apples to be ready for harvest.

It didn't take long to find *Mamá* and the children. Rosa could hear their voices long before she saw them.

Juan saw her first. "Rosa's here! Rosa's here!" he shouted. He and Graciela ran to meet their big sister. Lady raced around in circles when she saw Rosa. In one swoop, Rosa picked up Juan and reached over to pet Lady's silky mane.

"What are you doing out here, Lady?" she said.

Graciela answered for the dog. "Mr. Jones was out here talking to *Papá,* and Lady stayed with us after he left."

Rosa walked over to the ladder where *Papá* was picking Red Delicious apples. "What did Mr. Jones say about the job, *Papá?*"

"He doesn't know yet if there will be work."

"Oh." Rosa didn't know what to say to *Papá.* She wanted to stay in Washington more than anything she had ever wanted, but she was too shy to tell *Papá* her feelings. It would be wonderful if she could stay in school for a few more months. She thought of her friend Betty and of Betty's brother Jerry. She didn't want to leave them. She loved her teacher and the Christian school. If only her *Papá* could get work.

Mamá walked over to the apple bin and carefully emptied her picking bag. "Rosa, could you take Graciela and Juan for a walk? It's hard to keep an eye on them and pick at the same time."

"All right, *Mamá*." Rosa grabbed hold of her brother's and sister's hands and steered them down the row of apple trees. Juan ran ahead, with Lady following close behind. As they walked toward the rocky heights at the south end of the orchard, Lady suddenly began barking furiously. Rosa looked ahead. Juan stood near an irrigation pipe staring at something on the ground.

"Watch out!" Rosa screamed. "It's a snake!" She saw the diamond pattern on the back and the horny rings circling the rattlesnake's tail. Her heart pounded. "Stand still, Juan." Rosa's voice trembled with fear.

With eyes as big as marbles, Juan turned to look at his sister. He stayed where he was, but the dog ran toward the snake. Rosa grabbed Juan and pulled him back, yelling at Graciela to stay behind her.

Lady dashed back and forth, coming nearer and nearer to the snake. "Come here, Lady! Please come here!" Ignoring Rosa, Lady darted toward the snake. With one quick motion, the rattler struck, its fangs shooting venom into the dog's leg. Lady yelped.

"Come here, girl," Rosa called. Lady, whimpering in pain, limped toward Rosa.

"Now what will I do?" Rosa knew that the dog needed immediate help. The poison would spread quickly, and Lady needed a shot from the veterinarian.

Rosa thought quickly. "I'll have to get help for Lady and get Juan and Graciela out of here."

"You children stay close beside me," she commanded. "I'm going to try to carry Lady back to where *Papá* is."

By this time it was obvious that the dog was in great pain. Rosa noticed that Lady's front leg was starting to swell. Rosa gently patted her on the back. "Good girl, just lie still and let me pick you up."

Lady seemed to sense that Rosa was trying to help her. She didn't resist being picked up. Rosa bent down and took a deep breath. She lifted the big dog in her arms and struggled back through the orchard. Graciela and Juan stayed close beside their big sister.

"Graciela, you run ahead and get *Papá*," Rosa gasped when they neared the section of the orchard where her parents were picking. "Juan, you stay with me."

Rosa didn't think she could carry Lady much farther. The dog seemed to get heavier by the minute. Just when she thought she couldn't hold out any longer, she saw *Papá* running toward her.

"*Papá, Papá,* help us!" she screamed. She put Lady into his arms and followed as her father carried the dog to their old van that was parked at the edge of the orchard. *Mamá* ran toward the van, pulling the younger children along beside her.

Papá laid Lady in the back of the van and started the motor. He drove as fast as possible toward the Joneses' house, making the tires squeal as he turned the corner into their yard. When Mrs. Jones heard the horn honking, she ran out of the house. "What's the matter?"

"Lady's been bit by a rattler. She needs to see the vet," *Papá* said. "My Rosita carried her out to where I was so she could get help."

"My husband isn't here, but if you'll put Lady in our pickup, I'll take her into Yakima."

"Do you need one of us to go along?" *Papá* asked.

"I'll go," Rosa said. "I hope Lady will be all right. I could hold her on my lap."

"That would be a help," said Mrs. Jones. "Let's go." Rosa climbed into the truck. *Papá* lifted Lady out of the van and placed her on Rosa's lap. Rosa noticed how much more the leg was swollen. She stroked Lady's long nose and talked softly to her. "Good girl; you'll be fine."

On the ten-mile trip into Yakima, Mrs. Jones asked Rosa how the snake happened to bite Lady. Rosa explained that she and the children were walking through the orchard with Lady when

Lady jumped at the rattlesnake. "Lady probably saved Juan from getting bit," Rosa said, as she patted the dog's soft fur. Juan would have been right on top of the snake if Lady hadn't got there first.

"And you saved Lady's life by carrying her to your father," Mrs. Jones said.

After the veterinarian gave an antivenin shot to the dog, Mrs. Jones brought her out to the waiting room where Rosa sat. Lady waved her tail briefly when she saw Rosa. "Will she be all right?" Rosa asked.

"The vet thinks she'll be fine, thanks to your quick thinking. If you hadn't brought her in, the venom would have spread and could have killed her."

Rosa ducked her head and petted Lady. She was glad that she was there when Lady needed her. Even more, she was glad that Juan wasn't the one bitten by the rattler.

Mrs. Jones took Rosa back to the cabin. She thanked her repeatedly for what she had done for Lady. Rosa petted Lady one more time and went into the cabin. *Mamá* was getting supper ready.

"How is Lady?" *Mamá* vigorously stirred the kettle on the stove as she looked at Rosa.

"The vet said she'll be fine." Rosa decided she might as well ask the question that was burning in her mind. "Can I go visit Cousin Elena this weekend?"

"I don't know," *Mamá* said. "We'll have to ask *Papá*. We might have to go back to Mexico soon. The picking is almost over."

Rosa's heart sank. "I thought Mr. Jones had a job for *Papá*."

"He isn't sure yet." *Mamá* gave the beans another hard stir. "*Papá* went to see Mr. Jones. Ask him when he comes in. He'll know more about it."

Rosa went outside. She wanted to meet *Papá* as soon as he came home. When she heard the van coming, she ran to meet it. Her father jumped out. "How is Lady?"

"She's all right. The vet said it might take a while for the swelling to go down, but she'll be better soon."

Papá put his arm around Rosa's waist. "You were a brave girl to carry Lady back away from the snake. I'm proud of you."

"*Papá,* I want to ask you something."

"What is it, my Rosita?"

Rosa wondered if she could say it without looking guilty. "I have a question to ask you."

"Well, ask me."

"Could I . . ." Rosa stammered. "Can I go visit Cousin Elena this weekend?"

"For the weekend? Why do you want to visit her for the whole weekend?"

"Oh, I don't know." Rosa hadn't thought this out. "I just want to go see her. I haven't had a chance to spend much time with her since she doesn't go to the same school that I go to."

Papá looked at Rosa. "We might have to go back to Mexico soon. The picking's nearly done."

"Oh, *Papá,* I thought you said you had a job with Mr. Jones."

"It didn't work out. I just talked to him and he doesn't have any work for me."

"Then we'll have to leave again, and I won't get to go to my school."

"I'm sorry, Rosa; that's just the way it is. But I'll let you go to visit your cousin. They'll be traveling back with us. If we have to leave this weekend, you can come with them and we'll get together on the road."

Mr. Gomez gave his daughter a quick hug. "One thing, though. You are not to go near the river. You hear me?"

Rosa couldn't look at *Papá*. "Yes, *Papá*, I hear you." She reasoned that she hadn't said she would stay away from the river. She just said she had heard him.

Papá opened the door to the cabin and they went inside. Rosa felt like crawling under the bed and never coming out. It wasn't fair! Just when she finally had a best friend, she had to move. She'd have to leave Betty and Jerry and her teacher and all her friends at school. Why didn't God work it out so *Papá* could get work and they could stay here?

"What's the matter, Rosa? You look like a thundercloud." *Mamá* set the kettle filled with beans on the table.

"*Papá* just told me we can't stay here after the apples are picked."

"Come help me get the children's tortillas filled." *Mamá* put her arm around Rosa. "I've found that it helps to keep busy when you feel sad."

"I feel worse than sad, *Mamá*. I feel like it's hopeless." Rosa picked up a tortilla. "I finally found a friend. Now I have to leave and go some place else where I won't know anybody."

"I know, Rosa. How well I know!" *Mamá* sighed. "It's the way our people have always lived. You just learn to live with it."

That night, Rosa lay on her bed on the floor, staring into the darkness. It wasn't fair! Other girls got to finish school in one place. Other girls had friends to play with and talk to every day. She had to leave her friends behind and move to another place. She was glad that she had made plans to stay with Betty this weekend. At least she would have that time to be with her friend and her friend's brother. She had to admit that she wanted to see Jerry, too.

One part of her felt guilty that she had lied to her parents about going to Elena's. Another side said that it would serve them right for making her leave her friends and go back to Mexico. Rosa tossed and turned. Usually she slept well on the floor, but tonight she couldn't get comfortable in any position. She was cold, too. Graciela had pulled the quilt over to her side. When Rosa heard the creak of her parents' bed, she knew that *Mamá* must be awake, too.

"Are you awake, *Mamá?*" she whispered.

"*Sí*, yes I am." *Mamá's* whisper was even quieter than Rosa's. "Don't wake your brother and sister, but put your sandals on and come to the washroom with me."

Outside in the light of the full moon the apple trees looked like soldiers lined up in straight rows with their arms reaching toward the sky. It was eerie. *Mamá* put her arm around Rosa. "I'm sorry you are so sad. I heard you rolling around on the floor."

"Oh, *Mamá,* I wish we could stay here."

"We can't stay. There is no work for *Papá,* and we can't keep warm in the cabin in the cold winters here in Washington."

70   Rosa

"I know." Rosa shivered in the night air. "I just wish things were different." She opened the washroom door for *Mamá* and turned on the light switch. The washroom was cold, too. Rosa was glad when they went back to the cabin.

"Remember, you still have your family, even if we have to leave." *Mamá* gave Rosa a hug. "We'll always be together."

"I do love you, *Mamá*, and *Papá* too," Rosa said. "I just need a friend."

Rosa opened the door. It felt good inside. Mamá had put a log into the stove before she went to bed, and the stove was still warm. The wood from the apple trees made a quick, hot fire, even if it did leave lots of ashes in the stove.

Rosa gently pulled the quilt over to her side. Graciela stirred in her sleep. Rosa covered her little sister and turned over. She wished she knew how to pray. Maybe she could talk to Betty's mother about it this weekend. Then, as she thought about the weekend, she felt bad again about deceiving her parents. She not only had let them think she was going to be with Elena, but she had lied to *Papá* about not going to the river. Betty had the picnic all planned and it included a hike along the river. What a mixed-up, crazy world it was!

Rosa wondered if she could ever get to know Jesus as intimately as some others at her school seemed to know Him. They talked about being saved from sin and talking to Jesus. Rosa didn't know what to do, but she knew there must be an answer somewhere.

She heard soft snoring behind the curtain and knew that *Mamá* slept. Rosa pulled the quilt up under her chin and finally drifted off to sleep too.

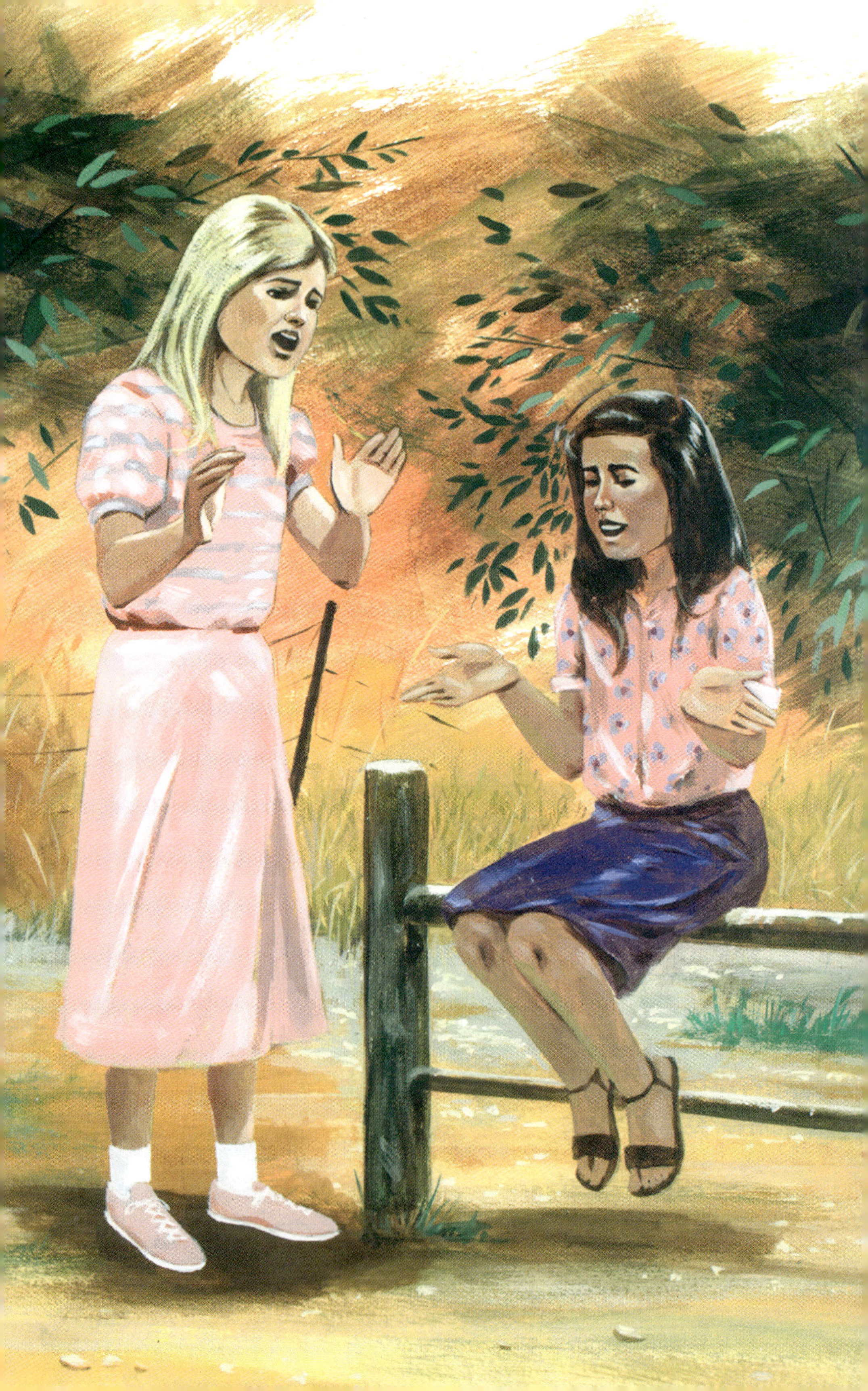

Chapter Six

THE PICNIC

Friday passed slowly in the classroom, and Rosa's thoughts were far from school lessons. She missed three words on the final spelling test. Usually she did well in math, but today she couldn't do anything right. All she could think about was having to leave her school and all her friends when she went back to Mexico.

At recess time she told Betty the news. "No, you can't go!" Betty screeched. "You're my best friend."

"I have to go with *Mamá* and *Papá*." Rosa ducked her head to hide her tears. "I want to stay here more than I have ever wanted anything before, but I can't. *Papá* is done picking, and there is no work." Suddenly a frightening thought came and she gasped aloud. "They might even leave this weekend while I'm at your house. What would I do then?"

"Oh, they won't go without you."

"They think I'm going to Elena's, and if the time comes to leave, I'm supposed to go with her family and meet *Papá* and *Mamá* on the road somewhere."

"Don't worry, we'll think of something," Betty said. "We'll walk past Elena's cabin on our way up the river tomorrow. We can tell if they're getting ready to leave."

The day finally ended. When the bell rang, Rosa gathered her books and climbed into the school van, relieved that the day was over.

"Rosa's coming to our house to spend the weekend," Betty told her father when he climbed into the driver's seat.

"Is that right?" Mr. Baker seemed surprised, but pleased. "What are you girls up to?"

"We're going on a hike along the river," Betty said. "I know the neatest place to have a picnic."

"Well, as long as you stay out of the river, you can go. There's a very strong current in most places. And you're not a swimmer."

"I know. We're not going swimming. I'm gonna pack a lunch, and we'll hike up toward that big rock that hangs out over the bank." Betty looked at Rosa. "We'll be careful, won't we, Rosa?"

Rosa nodded her head. She was so mixed up that she couldn't think straight. She really wanted to go with Betty, but she knew that she was disobeying her parents and also deceiving them.

When the van pulled up to the parsonage, Rosa saw Jerry putting his bicycle away in the garage. She felt her heart pounding. Why did she always feel this way whenever she saw him?

"Hi, Rosa," he called. "Mom told me you were going to stay overnight with us." He went inside the garage as Rosa and Betty headed toward the house.

Rosa looked around the huge living room. A piano stood in one corner with potted plants beside it. The sofa with its flowered print blended with matching chairs. Rosa stepped on the soft brown carpet and thought of the bare wooden floor in the cabin. This one room was bigger than their whole cabin. For a minute Rosa questioned whether she should have come or not. Betty had told her she would let her wear some of her clothes, but Rosa felt out of place in such a beautiful home.

"Your house is so pretty," she finally said. "I have never been in such a nice one in my life."

"Really?" Betty said. "It's not any nicer than any of my friends' houses." She stopped, embarrassed. "Oh, Rosa, I'm sorry; I forgot about your cabin." She grabbed Rosa's arm. "Let's go up to my room and change into something cooler. It's pretty warm."

Rosa followed Betty up the stairs. She thought how great it would be to have a room of her own. Probably *Mamá* was starting to fix the tortillas for supper about now. She wondered if Graciela and Juan were in *Mamá's* way.

"Your room is pretty," Rosa said. She wondered if pretty was a strong enough word. Frilly white curtains hung at the windows, matching the bedspread on the double bed. Over the bed was a canopy. Rosa had seen pictures of a canopy bed but never the real thing. To think that she would get to sleep under the canopy tonight was almost too much to comprehend.

She walked over to the dressing table and examined the mirror and things on top of the table. Betty's collection of stuffed animals hung in a net over the mirror. Again Rosa thought of Juan and his one little stuffed horse that he played with every day. He and Graciela wouldn't know what to do with so many toys. It was hard to keep from feeling envious of the pretty things in the room.

Then Betty opened her closet door, and Rosa saw dresses, tops, and skirts of all colors and styles. Betty picked out a jumper for Rosa, and a tee shirt. "Here," she said. "Try these on for size."

When the girls had changed clothes, they went to see if Mrs. Baker and Timmy were home. Jerry sat in front of the television. "Where's Mom?" Betty asked.

"She went to the store just before you came and took Timmy with her. She said she'd be right back."

Rosa and Betty went to the kitchen. Again Rosa was overwhelmed by the beautiful appliances. She couldn't help comparing the Bakers' electric stove with little "Midget" that her mother cooked on every day.

"Let's see what's in the refrigerator that we can fix for our lunch tomorrow," Betty said. "Here's some lunch meat and apples. I think Mom made cookies, too. We should make out all right."

Later, after supper, Mr. Baker called the family together. "Rosa, we always have family devotions in the evening," he explained. "We read the Bible and pray together. We'd be happy to have you join us."

Rosa and Betty sat on the sofa, Jerry and Timmy on the floor, and Mr. and Mrs. Baker in the plush chairs. After the pastor read a chapter from the Bible, he prayed for each member of the family, and for Rosa. "Please protect the girls as they go on their hike tomorrow," he said, as he ended his prayer. "Keep them in your care and help us to please you and obey you in everything that we do."

Betty and Rosa followed Timmy and Jerry up the stairs. In the upstairs hall Jerry stopped to talk to Rosa as Betty went on into her bedroom. "How do you say 'I'll see you later' in Spanish? Is it 'hasty luego'?"

Rosa smiled. "You have it almost right. It's *hasta luego*."

"Well, *hasta luego*, Rosa," Jerry said. "I'll see you later."

He went on down the hall and into his bedroom and shut the door. Rosa stood silent for a few minutes. What a neat guy he was! She felt even worse about leaving when she thought about Jerry.

When the girls were in bed, Rosa looked around the room. Bright moonlight streamed through the window, illuminating the white curtains and ruffled top of the canopy. "I can't believe I'm really here," she said. "It seems like a dream."

Betty reached over and hugged her friend. "I'm glad you came. I thought for a while you were gonna chicken out."

"I don't like it that *Mamá* and *Papá* think I'm at Elena's tonight," Rosa said. "I wish I didn't have to lie to them."

"We'll stop and see Elena tomorrow. Don't worry. They'll never know the difference."

Betty talked on and on into the night. Once in a while Rosa responded, but usually she let Betty do the talking. Finally it was quiet and Rosa knew that Betty slept. Rosa couldn't get to sleep. The bed seemed too soft after sleeping on the floor for so long. She tossed and turned, trying to get comfortable. She wondered if Graciela missed her tonight. She thought about *Mamá* and *Papá,* and the lie she had told them. Then she thought about Mr. Baker's prayer when he talked to God about obedience. She wished she could have talked to the pastor about what it meant to have your sins forgiven. As the night wore on, Rosa's troubled mind finally was quieted in sleep.

The first rays of sunshine crept through the window and landed on Rosa's face. Where am I? she wondered, as she woke with a start. Then she remembered. She was in Betty's bedroom. She looked at her friend, asleep beside her. Betty's face seemed whiter in the pale morning light. Her blond hair lay on the pillow like twisted straw.

Rosa quietly slid over the edge of the bed. She tiptoed down the hall, past Jerry's and Timmy's bedrooms, and into the bathroom. It was good to have a bathroom inside the house. She looked into the mirror. Her long black hair was tousled and snarled. Dark circles surrounded her eyes. She wondered if *Mamá* had stayed awake last night, too. Thinking of *Mamá* brought back the feelings of guilt. *Mamá* had been so strict about her not going to the river! Maybe she shouldn't have come to Betty's house. She headed back toward the bedroom. Betty was putting on her slippers.

"Oh, there you are," Betty said, as Rosa came into the room. "I wondered if I had just dreamed that you were here."

"I'm here," Rosa said.

"You're kind of quiet this morning. Is something wrong?"

"No," Rosa said. "I just feel bad that I had to lie to *Mamá* and *Papá*. They think I'm at my cousin's house."

"They won't care. You can tell them later what a good time you had with me. We'll pack our lunch and get going right after breakfast. It looks like a beautiful day for a picnic." Rosa looked out the window. It was a typical morning for late September in eastern Washington, with bright sunshine, blue sky, and clear air.

After breakfast, the girls loaded their basket with sandwiches, cookies, and apples. They filled a thermos with Kool-aid and lots of ice cubes. Four-year-old Timmy watched them pack the food. "Can I go along?" he asked.

"No, Timmy, you can't come with us. We're gonna hike for several miles," Betty said. "You'd never keep up."

Timmy went to his mother and grabbed her arm. "Please, Mommy, can I go with them? I'll be good. I'll stay with Betty all the time."

Mrs. Baker looked at her daughter. "Would you be willing to take him? I promised your dad I'd help clean the church this afternoon. I think Timmy could keep up with you."

Betty gave an exaggerated sigh. "I suppose we can take him if we have to." She turned to her little brother. "Get your sneakers on if you have to go with us."

Mrs. Baker made an extra sandwich and put another apple and more cookies in the basket. She gave all three of the children a hug as they started out the door. "Be careful, Timmy, and stay close to Betty and Rosa. They're in charge of you today. Be sure you mind them."

"I will, Mommy. Bye-bye."

Rosa looked around for Jerry, but he was nowhere in sight. He and Mr. Baker must have gotten up early this morning and gone somewhere. Or else they were still sleeping. She wanted to know but didn't have the courage to ask Mrs. Baker.

When the three children got to the river, they walked along the banks for about a half mile until they came to the cabin where Elena and her family stayed.

Rosa knocked on the door, but no one was there. "I wonder where they are," she said. "The door is padlocked." The children walked around the cabin, but there was no sign of Elena or her family.

"Maybe they went shopping," Betty said. "They'll probably be here later. We can stop on our way back."

The children walked on up the river until they found a flat stone that would do for a table. "What a perfect spot!" Betty said, as she put the basket down on the ground. "Feel that warm sun coming down through the pine trees. Aren't you glad you came?"

Rosa picked up a long branch from the ground and swept a spot for them to sit. "Yes, it is nice," she said.

"I'm hungry," Timmy said. "Let's eat."

"I suppose we could eat," Betty said. "Rosa, you get the sandwiches out and I'll pour the juice."

When everything was ready, the children sat on the ground and bowed their heads while Betty asked the blessing. Rosa was amazed again at the ease with which Betty prayed. She looked up through the trees. Not a cloud in the sky. She wondered where God lived. Did He have a home? Could He see them right now? So many unanswered questions filled her mind.

They ate their sandwiches and nibbled the cookies. "Let's take our apples with us and leave our basket here and hike up to where that big rock is," Betty said. She pointed ahead to where a huge rock jutted out above the river. White water swirled below as it rushed over the rocks. Sharp, dark rocks lined the bank.

They started walking. Rosa carried the branch she had used for a broom. "Just in case of snakes," she said. She couldn't forget the terrible experience when the rattler bit Lady. *Papá* had told her later that the best thing to do in "snake country" is to make noise with your feet, since snakes have good hearing but don't see well. He said they usually get out of your way when they hear you coming.

"Why are these rocks so black?" Rosa asked.

"That's volcanic rock," Betty said. "Years ago there was a ring of volcanoes all around this area. Some of them erupted and covered the ground with lava. This is what's left."

The girls, busy talking, hadn't noticed that Timmy was not with them. "Look!" Rosa shrieked, when she looked up. "He's headed for the big rock."

"Timmy, stay with us!" Betty shouted. It was like shouting at the rocks. Her active brother ignored her and ran ahead as fast as his chubby legs could carry him.

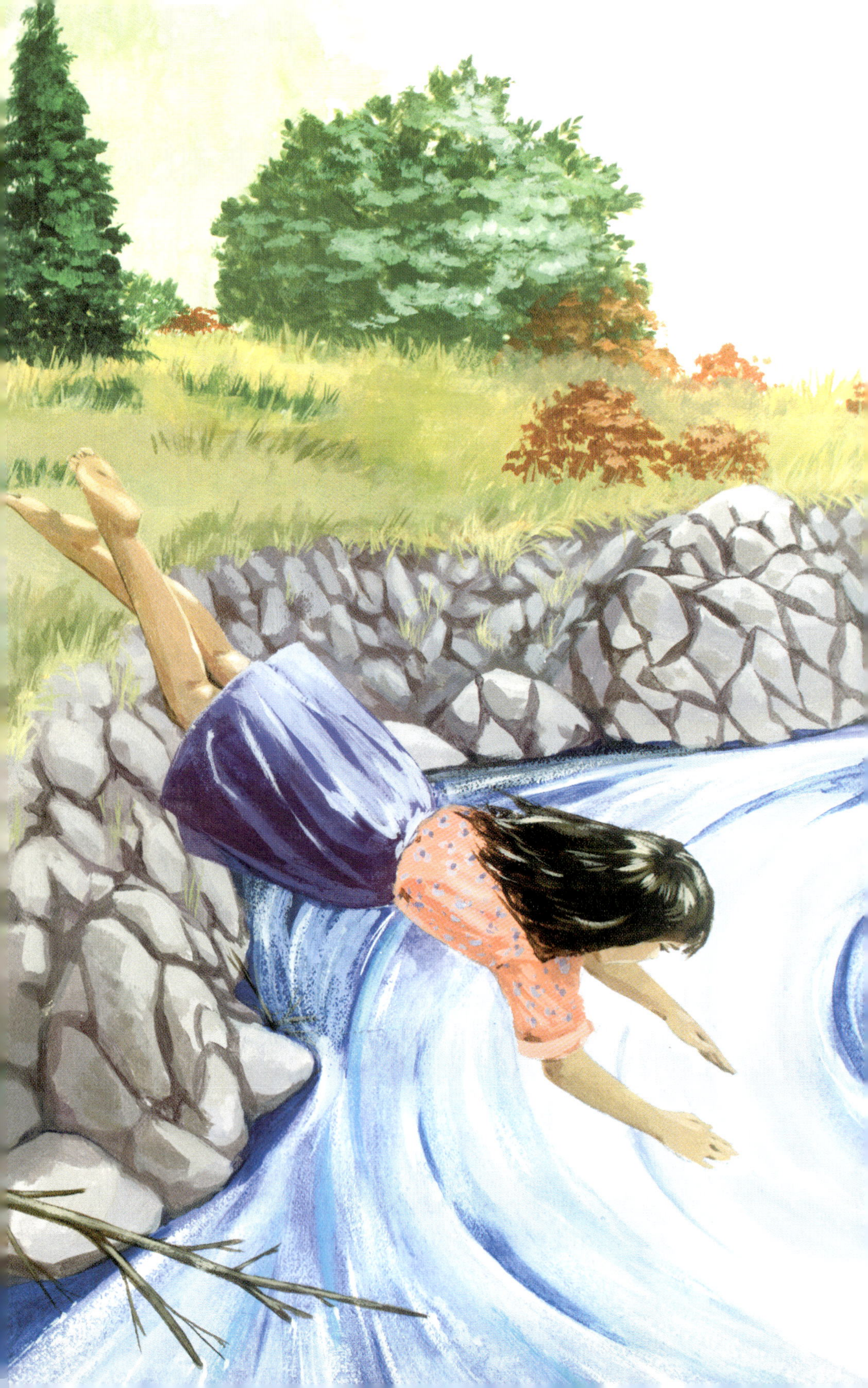

Chapter Seven

ROSA TO THE RESCUE

The girls took off, running as fast as they could, but Timmy was already climbing up the high rock. "Look at me," he yelled. "I'm Superman." He put his arms up and pretended to be flying through the air. Racing on the top of the rock, he skidded to a stop at the edge facing the river. He ran back and forth, going closer to the edge each time.

"Watch out, Timmy!" Betty screamed in terror. But it was too late.

Suddenly Timmy's feet slipped and with a sharp cry he plummeted to the water below, hitting the steep side of the rock as he fell.

"He can't swim," Betty gasped, "and I can't either."

Rosa kicked off her sandals and ran for the river. Without hesitating, she jumped into the icy water, then gasped for breath as she surfaced in the cold stream. Struggling against the current, she swam toward the little boy. "I'm coming, Timmy," she shouted.

For an instant she lost contact with the child as he sank under the water. When he surfaced again she grabbed his arm and pulled him toward her. Timmy fought against her, terrified, his arms flailing as he struggled to stay afloat. He choked on the water he had swallowed.

"Hold still," Rosa screamed. "You'll drown us both." Throwing her arm around his neck, she turned him on his back, and with the other arm swam for shore. The frightened boy screamed and fought, but Rosa hung on. It was all she could do to keep her head above water and hold on to Timmy, but she did it.

Meanwhile, Betty ran and grabbed the broken branch that Rosa had earlier used for a broom. She ran toward the river and held the branch over the bank, leaning out as far as she could. Rosa reached for the branch and missed. The current carried the struggling children down the river.

Betty ran along the bank, crying out, praying aloud, and stretching the stick as far as she could reach. Again Rosa grabbed for the branch and missed, but on the next try she got the tip of it in her fingers. She held on, thankful that the branch didn't break. Betty pulled them to where Rosa could touch bottom, and then Betty came into the water and lifted Timmy out onto dry ground while Rosa climbed the bank.

The wet, shivering children lay down in the hot sun. Rosa gasped for breath. "I . . . I . . . didn't think we were going to make it."

"Oh, Rosa!" Betty cried. "You saved Timmy's life. I was praying so hard for both of you. You were so brave!" She went over and hugged her friend. "Thank you, thank you, thank you! I thank God, too, for helping us. I couldn't have stood it if anything had happened to Timmy." She looked at her brother, "Even if it was his fault."

"Oh, you've got a cut on your foot," Betty cried, when she saw Rosa's foot. "And Timmy's legs are all scraped and bleeding. What can we do?"

Rosa looked around. What could they use? Then she saw some willow trees near the water's edge, their branches trailing almost in the river. She remembered the time when *Mamá* was making baskets out of willow twigs and cut her hand and she used willow leaves for a temporary bandage. "Get some leaves from that big willow tree beside the river," she said. "We'll make bandages out of them."

Betty tore several twigs off the willow and tied them together. She wrapped one bunch around Timmy's leg, while he yelled with pain, and gave the others to Rosa for her foot. Rosa jammed her sandal over the leaves to hold them tight over the cut. As soon as the bleeding stopped, the children started back over the volcanic rocks and down the trail along the river. When they picked up the picnic basket, Betty said, "I wanted it to be a great picnic, and now it's all spoiled. I'm sorry, Rosa."

"It's all right," Rosa said. "It's my fault too. I shouldn't have disobeyed my parents."

Limping, the exhausted children headed back toward the road. When they came to Elena's cabin, there still was nobody there. Not a sign of life showed anywhere. Outside the cabin was a pile of tin cans, and two rusty metal chairs leaned against the front step. The children tried to look in the window, but it was boarded up.

"I hope they haven't gone back to Mexico," Rosa said. She hurt so much and was so tired that she didn't want to even think about the possibility, but it stuck in her mind.

On the way home, Betty said, "You're a heroine, Rosa. When people hear about this you might even get a medal or something."

"I don't want a medal. I don't want my *Mamá* and *Papá* to know that I came to the river," Rosa said. "They would feel very bad that I disobeyed them."

"I can't walk any farther," Timmy said. "My legs hurt."

"I guess we'll have to carry you, then," Betty said. "Can you help me, Rosa?"

The girls made a seat with their hands. Rosa grabbed her arm with one hand and Betty's arm with the other. Betty did the same. Squatting down, they put their arms under the tired little boy and lifted him between them. They put the picnic basket over Timmy's arm. "This is a fireman's carry, Timmy," Betty said. "We learned about it in school. Just hang on to our shoulders, and we'll get you home."

Step by step Rosa struggled to keep going. Her foot hurt, and now her arms ached. Timmy seemed to get heavier and heavier as they walked along.

The dejected little group trudged on down the riverside path until they came to the road. "Wouldn't it be great if Dad would come along about now?" Betty said. Raising her shoulder up, she wiped the damp perspiration from her face with her shirt sleeve.

The children had walked about a quarter of a mile on the blacktop road when a pickup truck passed them. The driver swerved the truck to a stop by the side of the road and backed up. A woman got out and came toward the children. A big brown and gold dog trotted alongside.

"It's Mrs. Jones and Lady!" said Rosa. "Mrs. Jones will help us." Lady's tail wagged furiously when she heard Rosa's voice. She ran up to Rosa and began licking her hand.

"Whatever happened to you all?" asked Mrs. Jones. Rosa looked down at Timmy. Blood was seeping out from under the leaves that were wrapped around his leg. Her foot was a mess, too. Did she dare tell what had happened? Would Mrs. Jones tell her parents that she had been down by the river? She had just decided to tell her the truth when suddenly a look of surprise came over Mrs. Jones's face. "Rosa, what are you doing here? Why didn't you go with your parents?"

"Go where?" Rosa asked, with a sinking feeling inside.

"Why, back to Mexico, of course. Didn't you know that they left this morning?"

Rosa and Betty set Timmy down on the ground. He started to cry. Rosa felt like crying, too. "I didn't know they left," she said. "I stayed overnight with Betty. But *Mamá* and *Papá* thought I was with Elena. They wouldn't have gone without me. What will I do now?" The despair in her voice made it sound like a wail.

"Well, the first thing," Mrs. Jones said, "is to take care of your foot and this boy's injuries." She leaned over and examined Timmy's leg. "He has a deep cut on his right leg. I'll take you home so you can get your cuts taken care of; then we'll talk about what to do next."

Timmy started to yell when he heard her mention that he had a deep cut. With Betty's help, Mrs. Jones lifted the four year old and placed him in the cab of the pickup. Rosa and Betty crowded in beside him, and Lady jumped in at their feet.

"The last time you rode with me you saved Lady's life," Mrs. Jones said. "I'm glad I came along when I did today so I could help you."

"When did my parents leave?" Rosa asked.

"Oh, I'd say it was about ten o'clock this morning. The picking ended yesterday, and your family packed their van last night. I went over to say goodbye to them this morning. In fact, I asked about you, and they said you would be coming with your cousin."

"We must have just missed Elena and her family when we went by their cabin today," Rosa said. "Of course, they could have gone earlier and planned to meet *Mamá* and *Papá* somewhere tonight when they stopped." A discouraged look came over her face. "Sometimes they drive all night and meet the rest of the group the next morning. They could be clear in California before they miss me."

"Well, I'm sure they'll come back when they find out you're missing." Mrs. Jones smiled reassuringly at Rosa.

Betty had been very quiet throughout the conversation. Now she spoke. "It's just like the story of Jesus when he was twelve. His parents left him behind, thinking he was with the other relatives. That's what happened to you."

Rosa's thoughts were sad. She knew that Jesus had been obedient to his parents, and she hadn't. She wished she had listened to her *Papá* and stayed away from the river.

"Don't worry, Rosa," Betty said. "You can stay with us until they come and get you. It's really my fault that you got left behind. I'm so sorry I persuaded you to do wrong." She gave Rosa's arm a squeeze. "Anyway, I'm glad you get to stay with me a little longer."

Mrs. Jones drove her truck into the parsonage driveway. Jerry was mowing the grass. He looked up in surprise when he saw his sister and Rosa getting out of the pickup. Mrs. Jones walked around the truck and lifted Timmy out of the cab. Jerry stopped the mower and ran toward them. "What happened?"

"Rosa saved Timmy's life," Betty said. "Timmy fell off the big rock into the river, and Rosa jumped in and rescued him. She's a good swimmer, and really brave. You should have seen her jump into that icy water."

"Betty was brave too," said Rosa. "She was afraid of the water, but she pulled us out with a tree branch."

"I was scared," Timmy interrupted. "Then Rosa grabbed my neck and pulled me up so I didn't swallow any more water."

Rosa saw the look of gratitude that came over Jerry's face. She wondered what she looked like. Probably like a drowned rat. She hoped Jerry wouldn't notice her stringy hair and her dirty feet.

When Mr. and Mrs. Baker came home from cleaning the church and heard the story, they, too, were grateful to Rosa for her bravery. Everyone talked excitedly about what had happened and how brave Rosa was. She and Timmy were the center of attention, but the more they praised her the worse Rosa felt. She didn't have the courage to tell them what had really happened. They didn't know that she had lied to her parents.

That night the Baker family gathered for family devotions. "Rosa, we are very thankful for what you did for Timmy," Mr. Baker said. "You will always have a special place in our hearts."

"If you hadn't gone along today, we would have lost our Timmy," Mrs. Baker said. "We thank God that Betty has such a good friend as you."

Rosa couldn't take it any longer. She knew that she had to tell them the truth. "I'm not as good as you think," she said. "I disobeyed my parents and lied to them. I told them I was with my cousin this weekend. Now *Mamá* and *Papá* have gone back to Mexico," she sobbed. "And they think I'm with Elena."

"Let's pray about it," Mr. Baker said. After he read Bible verses, he thanked God for watching over the children that day. He especially thanked God for Rosa. He prayed that God would work the problem out and that her parents would come back soon. He prayed that Rosa might know Jesus as her Friend and Savior.

"Tomorrow is Sunday. We'd like to invite you to go to Sunday school and church with us," he said to Rosa after he finished praying. I'll go over to the cabin tonight and leave a note on the door, so when your parents come back they'll know where to find you. I'll talk to the Joneses, too, in case they check with them."

Mrs. Baker came over to where the girls sat and put her arm around Rosa's shoulder. "Don't worry, dear. God loves you, and He will help you. Just trust Him. He wants to be your best friend."

Long after the girls had showered and climbed into bed that night, Rosa was awake. She thought about the day's happenings. She was glad that she could rescue Timmy, but she didn't feel like a heroine. She felt bad that she had disobeyed *Mamá* and *Papá*. Not only had she disobeyed them, but she had lied as well. If only there was a way she could make it right. She wished they were here now so she could tell them she was sorry.

As the moonlight filtered across the bed, Rosa decided that she would try to be a better girl from now on. Maybe if she worked at it she could remember to always obey and tell the truth. But it was hard to do by herself. She thought about Mr. Baker's prayer. What did he mean about Jesus being a friend and Savior? And Mrs. Baker had said that Jesus wanted to be her best friend. Could Jesus really be her friend? God wouldn't like someone who had lied and disobeyed, would He? It was too much to think about tonight. She was so tired, and her foot hurt. She thought about going to church tomorrow. It had been a long time since she had been in a church service. What would she wear? The clothes she had worn today were dirty and torn. Restlessly she turned over and tried to get comfortable. She missed *Mamá* and *Papá*. Where were they tonight? Did they know yet that their daughter was missing?

Rosa looked out the window from where she lay in bed. The moonlight streamed inside, lighting up the room almost like daylight. "God, are you awake?" she whispered. "Please help me." There was no audible answer, but Rosa felt a faint hope beginning in her heart. Finally, her eyes closed and she slept.

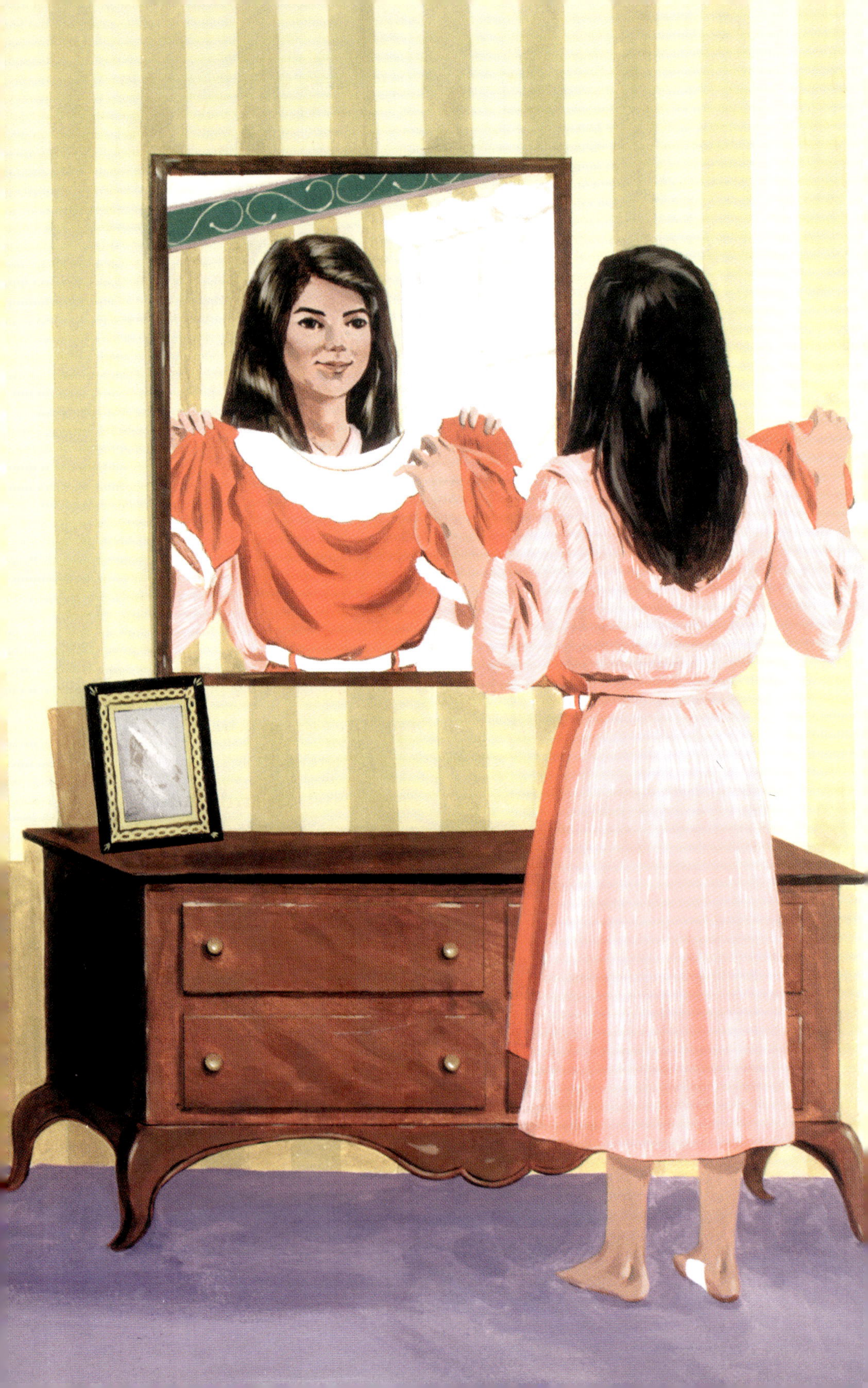

Chapter Eight

A FRIEND FOREVER

The twinge of pain in her foot woke Rosa. At first she wondered if she had bumped her toe on the bedrail. When she pulled the covers to one side and saw the clean bandage on her foot, she remembered the traumatic experience of yesterday. She trembled. What if she couldn't have gotten Timmy out of the river? She was thankful that they were both safe. Just thinking about the rushing water and the pull of the current frightened her.

Another dark thought entered her mind. *Mamá* and *Papá* would find out about her disobedience today if they came back. She wanted to see her parents and be with them as soon as possible, but she knew she would be in trouble when she did see them.

"Wake up, girls," Mrs. Baker called up the stairs. "Time to get ready for church."

Betty opened her eyes and looked over at Rosa. "Are you awake?"

"*Sí*, I mean, yes," Rosa said. "I've been awake for a long time."

"Is your foot bothering you?"

"*Un poco*, a little. There's some pain, but I can stand it." Rosa gingerly placed her feet on the carpet and put on the bathrobe that Betty had lent her. She used one of Betty's combs to get the tangles out of her long hair.

"Let me get a dress for you." Betty hopped out of bed and opened the closet door. "How about this red one with the full skirt? I think it would look good on you, with your dark hair."

"Oh, Betty, it's beautiful." Rosa held the dress in front of her and looked in the mirror. The dark red color reflected in her cheeks and contrasted well with her tan skin. Reluctantly she took her eyes off the dress and turned to Betty. "What are you wearing?"

"I think I'll wear this blouse and skirt." Betty held up a navy blue skirt and light blue top. "It looks like it's going to be another warm day."

When the girls came down to the breakfast table, Rosa was aware of Jerry looking at her. She was glad for Betty's dress that fit her so well. "How's your foot?" he asked.

"Much better," Rosa said. "*Gracias,* I mean, thanks," she quickly added, sitting down at her usual place at the table.

"You don't have to apologize," Jerry said. "I like to hear your Spanish."

"Rosa, would you like to ask the blessing before we eat?" Mr. Baker asked after all the family was seated.

Rosa's face blanched. "I . . . I . . . I don't think I could." she stammered. "*Lo siento*, I mean, I'm sorry."

"That's all right," Mr. Baker said. "Let's pray."

The others seemed to enjoy their meal after the prayer, but Rosa had trouble swallowing her pancakes. It seemed as if a lump as big as a softball was lodged in her throat. She knew that the Bakers were her friends, but she felt as lonely as though she were all by herself out along the river. Even Betty seemed distant. Rosa knew it must be only in her mind, because Betty hadn't said or done anything different.

Rosa was quiet on the way to church, sitting between Betty and Jerry. Once she sneaked a look at Jerry and saw him looking back at her. He smiled. Rosa pretended she was looking out the window. "Look, Timmy," she said to the four-year-old in the front seat, "There's where Mrs. Jones picked us up yesterday."

"I was sure glad to have her come along," Betty said. "Timmy felt like he weighed a ton."

"What's a ton?" Timmy asked.

"Two thousand pounds."

"I'm not that much," Timmy said.

"Well, you felt like it to us. Didn't he, Rosa?"

"What?" Rosa turned toward Betty. "I'm sorry, I wasn't listening."

"You looked like you were miles away. What are you thinking about anyway?"

"*No sé.*"

"What does 'no say' mean?"

Rosa chuckled. "It means 'I don't know.'"

"We're almost there," Mrs. Baker said. "Rosa, I teach the fifth and sixth graders in Sunday school, so you and Betty will be in my class."

"*Está bien,* that's fine."

Mr. Baker parked under the shade of a maple tree, and everyone went into the church. Rosa recognized many of her classmates as she and Betty joined them in the opening session of Sunday school. They sang some choruses and songs that she had learned at school. When they sang "I Have Decided to Follow Jesus," Rosa's thoughts went back to the night of the program, when the cat had walked in during her solo. It was funny how she could smile about it now when it had seemed so terrible at the time.

"This will be Rosa's last Sunday with us," Mrs. Baker announced to the boys and girls when they gathered in her classroom. She is going back to Mexico with her parents. We'll miss her."

"Not as much as I'll miss you," Rosa said. "I don't want to leave. I really like it here, and I love my school and my friends."

"This morning I'd like to talk about our best friend," Mrs. Baker said. "I feel that perhaps someone here needs to hear what Jesus did for us when he died on the cross for us."

Rosa sat up straighter in her chair. Maybe she would find out what it meant to be a follower of Jesus.

"In the book of John we read that Jesus said, 'Ye are my friends, if ye do whatsoever I command you.' " Mrs. Baker looked from one pupil to the other. "So, how can we be a friend of Jesus?"

"By obeying Him," said a girl sitting near the door.

"And what has He told us to do?"

"Well," Betty said, "He told us to love one another."

"He told us to love God with all our heart, our soul, and our mind and our strength," said a boy.

"He told us to believe in Him," said another boy.

"Who knows a Bible verse about that?" asked Mrs. Baker.

"How about John 3:16?" said a girl.

"Yes," said Mrs. Baker, "let's say it together. We probably all know it by heart."

Most of the class joined in saying the verse. "For God so loved the world, that He gave His only begotten Son that whosoever believeth in Him should not perish, but have everlasting life."

The class was still as Mrs. Baker continued. "Isn't it wonderful that Jesus came to earth and died for us so that our sins could be forgiven, and so that He could be our best friend?"

Rosa sat quietly, in deep thought. Could it be true that God loved her so much that He let His Son Jesus die for her sins? She thought of the lies she had told and her disobedience to her parents. She felt as if her heart would break when she thought of God loving her so much and how she had failed Him.

When the bell rang, Rosa stayed in the room after the other children left. Mrs. Baker turned toward her and asked the question that Rosa had wanted to hear.

"My dear Rosa, would you like to give your heart to Jesus and let Him forgive you? He wants to be your best friend."

Tears streamed down Rosa's cheeks. "Yes, I would like that very much, but I don't know what to say."

Mrs. Baker put her arm around Rosa's shoulder and led her to a chair. She closed the classroom door. "I'll help you," she said, as she opened her Bible to Romans 3:23. Carefully explaining the Scriptures, Mrs. Baker showed Rosa how all have sinned, and how Jesus died for all. "The Bible tells us in Romans 10:13, 'For whosoever shall call upon the name of the Lord shall be saved.'"

"Whosoever means you, Rosa. All you have to do is confess your sins to Jesus. He will hear you, and He will forgive."

"But how do I confess?" Rosa asked.

"Just tell Jesus that you are sorry for what you have done and that with His help you will not do it again."

Rosa bowed her head. She felt so sorry for her sins! "I'm sorry, Jesus," she whispered. "Please forgive me for lying, and for disobeying my parents, and for everything else bad that I have done."

A great sense of peace and forgiveness came into Rosa's heart as she reached out in faith and accepted forgiveness and believed in Christ as her Savior. "Oh, thank you, Jesus," she said. "I love you."

"Where is Jesus, now?" asked Mrs. Baker, when Rosa had finished praying.

Rosa thought for a minute. "He's with me." A big smile broke over her face. "He is my friend now."

Mrs. Baker opened her Bible to the last chapter, and the last verse, of the book of Matthew. "Look here, Rosa," she said. "Read what this says. It's Jesus' words to his followers."

" 'Lo, I am with you alway, even unto the end of the world,' " Rosa read.

"Jesus will never leave you, wherever you go, Rosa. He is your very best friend. In fact, in the book of Proverbs it says that 'there is a friend that sticketh closer than a brother.' "

Rosa thought about her brother. Juan liked to be close to her. Imagine someone being closer than a brother! What a wonderful thing to happen to her! She had a friend who would never leave her, and He would be even closer to her than her family.

"Do you have your own Bible, Rosa?" Mrs. Baker asked.

"No, I don't have one."

"I'm going to give you this Bible that we've been reading from this morning," said Mrs. Baker. "You may keep it. Reading and obeying God's Word will help you grow spiritually."

"Thank you, Mrs. Baker, I'll read it every day."

Rosa went upstairs to the sanctuary, looking for Betty. She wasn't anywhere in the room. When Rosa went into the girls' restroom to rinse her face, Betty was just coming out the door. "Where have you been?" she asked. "What happened?"

"Oh, Betty," Rosa began to speak but couldn't continue. When she finally could control her voice, she told Betty about giving her heart to Jesus in the Sunday school classroom. "I am so happy, Betty; I know that I'll have a friend who will never leave me, and I'll never have to leave him."

Betty put her arms around Rosa. "I'm so glad, Rosa. I've been praying ever since you came that you would know Jesus as your Savior." The tears began to stream down her cheeks, too. "I'm sorry that I talked you into going with me yesterday. Will you forgive me?"

"*Sí*, yes, of course I forgive you." A little frown crossed Rosa's face. "I must ask my parents to forgive me, too. Do you suppose they will?"

"Now don't you start worrying already. You can ask your best friend, Jesus, to help you, and He will. You just wait and see.

"*Gracias*, Betty. Thanks for all your help, too."

During the worship service, Rosa followed in her Bible as the pastor read the Scriptures. Every word seemed alive. She hadn't realized how powerful God's Word really was. There was so much there to help her to live as a Christian.

When the service ended, Rosa looked for her schoolteacher. "I'm going to go back to Mexico when my parents get me," she said. "Thank you for everything you taught me."

"Oh, Rosa, we'll miss you so much." Mrs. Jenson gave Rosa a hug. "You have been a very special part of our class." She paused. "What about your school work? Will you be in school somewhere?"

"I don't know," Rosa said. "Sometimes it's a long time before we stay in one place long enough to go to school."

"I know what I'll do," Mrs. Jenson said. "We have some extra books in the storeroom. Come with me and I'll get them for you. You can study at home."

Rosa went to tell the Bakers where she would be, and then she followed Mrs. Jenson into the classroom. While her teacher was in the storeroom, Rosa looked around the familiar classroom. She would miss the cheerful place with its geraniums and books and desks. But most of all she would miss her teacher and her classmates.

She went to her desk and took out her notebook and pencils.

When Mrs. Jenson came out of the storeroom, her arms were loaded with books and workbooks. "Here, Rosa, take these with you. I'll see that they are paid for. There is at least a year's work here for you to do."

Tears welled up in Rosa's eyes. "You are so good to me," she said. "I'll miss you." She looked up at her teacher. "I asked Jesus to forgive me this morning after Sunday school. He is my best friend now."

"Oh, my dear, I am so proud of you." Mrs. Jenson put her arms around Rosa and hugged her tightly. "I'll be praying for you. Goodbye, and God bless you."

Rosa picked up the armload of books and walked to the Bakers' car, where the family was waiting. "Let me help you," Jerry said, as Rosa approached. He took the heavy load of books and placed them inside the car.

"What's all that?" Betty asked.

"Mrs. Jenson gave me books and workbooks so I can study on my own," Rosa said. "Maybe I can even help *Mamá* learn to read English."

When they arrived at the parsonage, Rosa squealed with joy, "Oh, there's *Papá's* van." The rusty van, with a box tied on top, waited on the street in front of the Bakers' home. As soon as Mr. Baker stopped the car, Rosa jumped out and ran toward her mother, who had gotten out of the van.

"*Mamá,* you did come back! You came back for me!" Rosa ran into *Mamá's* arms. "*Lo siento, Mamá*. I'm sorry I disobeyed you and went to the river with Betty. I wasn't with Elena at all. Please forgive me for lying to you and *Papá*." The tears streamed down her face. "Jesus forgave me for doing wrong; will you forgive me?"

Juan and Graciela slid out of the van and came to hug Rosa's legs. "Rosa, Rosa, we missed you."

Rosa reached down to hug her brother and sister. "I missed you, too."

Papá got out of his side of the van and came around to join the excited group. "Rosita, what happened? We got all the way to Portland before we found out that you weren't with your cousin."

"I'm so sorry, *Papá*. I lied to you. I really went with Betty when I said I was going with Elena. Please forgive me."

Papá tugged on his mustache. "It caused us a lot of extra miles of travel, besides the worry of where you were. You did wrong to tell us that story."

"It was a lie, *Papá*. I told you a lie, and I'm sorry. Jesus has forgiven me; will you forgive me?" Rosa hung her head, trying to keep *Papá* from seeing her tears.

"My Rosita," *Papá* put his arm around her trembling shoulder. "I forgive you, but what is this about Jesus?"

"Oh, *Papá,* He's my best friend now. I can't wait to tell you all about it."

Rosa was so absorbed in greeting her family that she hadn't noticed that the Baker family stood quietly waiting to be introduced. "I'm sorry, *Mamá* and *Papá,* this is Pastor and Mrs. Baker, and Betty and Jerry and Timmy."

"I remember the pastor and Betty," said Mr. Gomez. He put out his hand to shake hands with Mrs. Baker. "I'm glad to meet you. Thank you for taking care of our Rosa until we could get her.

All of a sudden it hit Rosa. This was goodbye. She went over to Betty and threw her arms around her friend. "Goodbye, Betty, I'll miss you so much. You are my next-to-best friend now."

Betty choked up. "I know what you mean. I'm glad you have Jesus as your best friend. I'll sure miss you. I'd write to you, but I don't know where to send a letter."

"I'll write to you when we get back in Mexico," Rosa said. "Oh, no," she said, "I've still got your dress on."

"You can have it to remember me by," Betty said.

"Oh, Betty, how could I ever forget you and your family?" Rosa looked at Jerry. "Goodbye, Jerry. Thanks for helping to carry my books."

"That's okay; I was glad to help such a neat girl." Jerry said.

Mr. and Mrs. Baker and Timmy each hugged Rosa, thanking her again for rescuing Timmy from the river. "Thank you for helping me to know Jesus," Rosa said. "I feel better about leaving, now that I know that Jesus will always be with me wherever I go."

"We'll pray for you every day," Mrs. Baker said. She gave her another hug and whispered in her ear, "Remember to read the Bible every day, and write and let us know how you're doing."

Then it was time to leave. The old van chugged down the road with Rosa waving her hand out the side window.

"*Adiós, amiga,*" Betty shouted.

"*Adiós, amiga,*" Rosa answered. "*Hasta luego.* See you later."